Silverspur;

The Mountain H

A Tale of the Arapaho Country

Edward Willett

Alpha Editions

This edition published in 2023

ISBN : 9789357933544

Design and Setting By
Alpha Editions
www.alphaedis.com
Email - info@alphaedis.com

Contents

CHAPTER I. MOUNTAIN MEN. ....- 1 -

CHAPTER II. A FOOT RACE................................- 7 -

CHAPTER III. THE GIRL WARRIOR. ....- 12 -

CHAPTER IV. THE PROPHET'S
CHILD ....- 16 -

CHAPTER V. THE SNAKE. ....- 21 -

CHAPTER VI. CONFESSION UNDER
TORTURE. ....- 26 -

CHAPTER VII. OLD BLAZE IN A
TIGHT PLACE. ....- 31 -

CHAPTER VIII. A LOVER'S
MEETING..- 36 -

CHAPTER IX. DOVE-EYE
DENOUNCED...- 41 -

CHAPTER X. THE FALSE PROPHET................- 45 -

CHAPTER XI. NOT UNWHIPT OF
JUSTICE. ....- 50 -

CHAPTER XII. "THE GOVERNOR." ....- 57 -

CHAPTER XIII. KATE ROBINETTE..................- 63 -

CHAPTER XIV. DIFFICULT NEGOTIATIONS. ....- 69 -

CHAPTER XV. KNIFE TO KNIFE. ....- 76 -

CHAPTER XVI. CONCLUSION. ....- 81 -

CHAPTER I.
MOUNTAIN MEN.

In a saloon adjoining the St. Louis theater (the city at that time could boast of but one theater) were collected half a dozen men, middle-aged and young. It was evident, even to a casual observer, that they were bound together by ties of friendship, or of interest, or of common pursuit; for they formed a knot by themselves, associating with no others, and their appearance was quite different from that of other frequenters of the saloon. Their dress was fine—not gaudy, but costly—and they wore their broadcloth with the air of men who had been born to it. Their manners were gentlemanly, if not refined, characterized by the frankness and high-toned independence that ought to distinguish the American citizen. Their tastes, also, were of a costly and luxurious nature. Disdaining the low-priced whisky and the fiery brandy that was chiefly dealt out at the saloon, they lavished their gold pieces upon the choicest wines, as freely as if they had owned mines of the precious metals. They were talking, when they entered the saloon, of the theater which they had just left; but their tone changed after a while, and the conversation was of mountains and plains, of Indians and buffalo, of wild scenes and daring exploits. They spoke of these subjects, so strange and wonderful to the uninitiated, as if they were matters of every-day occurrence, laughing and joking the most over the worst perils and the greatest hardships.

These men were objects of interest to a person who made his appearance in the saloon shortly after they entered it—a man past the middle age, grotesque, uncouth, and strangely out of place in those surroundings.

Although his features were peculiar enough, his dress was chiefly calculated to attract attention in a civilized community. His principal garment was a hunting-shirt of dressed deerskin, embroidered in the Indian fashion, and ornamented with a fringe of green worsted. A heavy cape was attached to this garment, and it was tied at the waist with a red worsted sash. The breast was open sufficiently to give a view of a red flannel shirt. Under the principal garment were leggings of deerskin, heavily fringed below the knee, until they were joined by a pair of moccasins. A cap made of the skin of the gray fox, with the tail prominent behind, and a silver medal set in the front, completed the attire of this strange personage.

His face and form were also peculiar. From under his cap fell straggling locks of black hair, thickly touched with gray. Beneath bushy eyebrows were set a pair of keen, sparkling and restless eyes. His nose, large, prominent, and shaped like the beak of the eagle, had been by some means turned awry, and its end pointed unmistakably toward the left side of his face. His mouth was large, but pleasant in expression, and his right cheek was remarkable for a purplish spot that covered the region about the cheek-bone. None of his other features were visible, being hidden by a heavy beard, of black mixed with gray, that flowed in a tangled mass to his breast. As to shape, he was a little above the medium hight, with very broad shoulders and breast and thence tapering down to his feet, which were big and broad enough to support the structure above them.

His left hand carried a long and heavy rifle, ancient and battered, worn by time and hard service. A knife with a buckhorn handle was stuck in a leather sheath in his sash, and his powder-horn and bullet-pouch hung at his side.

After watching the group of well-dressed men for a while, he stepped up to them.

"I heern tell that ye are mounting men, strangers," he said, "though I'm durned ef ye look a bit like it."

"You are not far wrong, my friend," replied a heavy set man, with a jovial countenance; who seemed to be the chief personage in the group. "We are generally called mountain men, though most of us belong to the plains, rather than the mountains."

"Ye're all fixed up so mighty fine, that I had my doubts, and I felt kinder skeery of ye; but I allowed I mought make bold to ax about suthin' I'm on the hunt of down hyar. Hope thar's no harm done."

"None to us, my friend. We are always glad to meet a mountain man in the settlements. Won't you take something to loosen your tongue?"

"Don't mind ef I do, cap., bein' it's you."

"Thunderation!" exclaimed the mountaineer, as the effervescent champagne bubbled out into a goblet before him. "Hev ye got a b'ilin' spring down hyar in St. Louis?"

"Drink it quick, my friend, before it dies."

"Wal, ef I must eat it alive, hyar's to ye!"

"Don't you like it?" was asked, as he sat down the glass, with a wry face.

"Cain't say that I really love the taste of it. It's most too sweetish to suit this child, and I'm afeard the crittur is never gwine to quit kickin'."

"Peter, give the old man some brandy, or any thing he may choose to call for. You said, my friend, that you wished to ask us about something that you are on the hunt of. We will be glad to help you."

"I allowed, bein's ye're mounting men, ye mought p'raps know suthin' of a young chap named Fred Wilder."

A young man in the group gave a slight start, and laid his hand on the shoulder of the gentleman who was about to reply.

"There are several men of that name in the city," he said. "Did the person you speak of ever pass by any other name?"

"The Injuns called him Silverspur, and he was ginerally called by that name in the mountings; but I allow he wouldn't wear it down hyar in the settlements. Thar's me, now; I've been called Old Blaze so long, and nothin' else, that I ain't raally sure whether I've got any other name."

"What sort of a man was he?"

"Wal, as fur looks, he was what is called a good-lookin' man, though I never took on much about his good looks, or thought they war any thin' to brag on. He was about your hight, and with jist such eyes, and nose and mouth the same to a dot. Durned ef you don't look a heap like him."

"Thank you for the compliment."

"But looks don't count in a skrimmage, and they ain't worth talkin' about. Thar's whar Silverspur did count, and he was as good a man in a tight place, fur his inches, as I ever sot eyes onto. Ye mought bet yer pile that he'd never ran away from a fight, or go back on a friend. He was the right kind of a man, and old Jule knows it."

The hunter slapped his rifle with his hand, to give emphasis to this assertion.

"Perhaps," suggested one of the gentlemen, "this Wilder is the same man who was hung last week, for horse-stealing."

"Ye're wrong thar, stranger," said the hunter, as his eyes flashed wickedly. "I won't say but ye may hev sech a notion; but I hope ye won't speak it out ag'in afore me. Silverspur warn't the kind of a man to git picked up as a hoss-thief."

"He is mistaken, my friend," said the young man. "I knew Silverspur; but he is dead."

"Dead! That chap! Dead!"

The hunter's rifle fell on the floor, with a crash that startled all in the room, and his countenance was expressive of the deepest sorrow, as he stared blankly at his informant.

"Ef Silverspur is dead, what's other folks livin' for? Seems that a man like him hain't no right to be took away. Thar's few enough like him, and old Jule knows it. Did he jest die, stranger, or mought suthin' hev happened to him?

"He was killed—shot in an encounter—here in St Louis."

"Some sort of a skrimmage ye mean, I reckon. Is the man who did it a-livin'?"

"There were several men. It was not known which of them fired the shot."

"Will ye be so kind, stranger, as to put me on the trail of these men?"

"What would you do?"

"Foller it up, ontil the last one of 'em is wiped out. They'll never shoot another man. Such a chap as Silverspur!"

"Come, Fred," remarked one of the party; "don't carry the joke too far."

"You take it too hard, my friend," said the young man, as the hunter's eyes filled with tears. "I may have been mistaken. In fact, Silverspur is alive and well. Why, Old Blaze! don't you know me?"

The hunter looked amazed. He seemed hardly to know whether to be angry or pleased; but gladness got the better of indignation, and his face fairly blazed with joy as he grasped the outstretched hand of the young man.

"The livin' thunder!" he exclaimed. "Who would ever hev thought that ye could fool this child so easy! It's plain enough now, though shavin' and ha'r-trimmin' and settlement fixin's do make a powerful differ."

"You will forgive me for my joke, I know, if you are really glad to see me."

"Glad! That ain't no word fur it boy. I've come all those many miles to see ye, and I reckon I ort to be glad to find ye, at the eend of such a long trail."

"What is the news in the mountains?"

"Wal, things go on purty much in the old way; but thar's suthin' turned up that I 'lowed ye'd want to know about."

"What is it?"

"That Injun gal. Hev ye forgot her a'ready?"

"Dove-eye? No indeed! You may laugh if you please, gentlemen; but this is a matter in which I am deeply interested."

"An affair of the heart," remarked one of the party. "I was spoony about a red-skin girl myself, when I was younger than I am now. We will leave you with Old Blaze, Fred. As he has come so far to see you, he must have something of importance to communicate."

The traders left the saloon, and Fred Wilder, leading the hunter to a seat, asked him concerning the news that he had brought.

"It's all about that Injun gal, I tell ye," replied Old Blaze. "It was White Shield who sent me—that Blackfoot friend of yours."

"Where is White Shield, and how is he? I would be right glad to see him."

"Ye'll never see him ag'in, in this world. That Injun's dead."

"You are not following my example, I hope, and trying to fool me."

"Not a bit of it. The Blackfeet got him. They were powerful mad because he quit the tribe and ran off with you and old Robinette's gal, and they were bound to kill him when they caught him. I happened to be on good terms with the riptyles jest then, and I saw White Shield afore he died. He told me about the Injun gal, and made me give him my solemn promise that I would hunt you out and let you know."

"How did they kill him?"

"Jest knocked him in the head, and left him to the buzzards."

"Poor fellow! It would have been better for him if he had never seen me. His friendship was fatal to him. What did he say about Dove-eye?"

"Yes, that is the gal's name, ef it ain't wrong to call a warrior a gal. Thar's precious little of the dove about her now, 'cordin' to what White Shield said. He was among the Crows, when they had a skrimmage with the 'Rapahoes, and he said that Dove-eye was about the wildest warrior the Crows had ag'inst them. Since she took to the war-paint, he said, the 'Rapahoes seemed to hev abundance of bad feelin' toward the Crows, and fou't 'em as ef they wanted to rub out the tribe."

"I thought she was dead. I sought her so long, without finding even a trace of her, that I could only suppose her to be dead. As she is living, I must seek her again. I must go to the West. White Shield never lied."

"I reckon you will soon see her, cap., ef you will stay with the Crows a while. It won't be long afore you will hev a chance to knock her in the head or take her prisoner, ef she don't git ahead of you in the fightin' business."

"Come to my lodge, Blaze, and stay with me while you are in town. In two days I can get ready, and then we will start for the mountains, if you are willing."

"Willin' and glad enough. I'm tired of this hyar settlement a'ready."

CHAPTER II.
A FOOT RACE.

Near the head of the Platte, more than a hundred miles beyond Fort Laramie, had encamped, one midsummer night, a party of hunters and trappers, among whom were Fred Wilder and Old Blaze.

The party numbered only a dozen men, and as their force was so small, they had taken special care to guard against attack or accident. Notwithstanding their precautions, they discovered, in the morning, that four of their best horses were missing, and a council was held to consider the matter.

As there were no signs of Indians to be seen, they came to the conclusion that the animals had got loose, and had taken the back track on the trail by which the party had come. As most of the men were in a hurry to reach their destination, they proposed to push forward without regarding the loss; but Wilder, to whom three of the horses belonged, was loth to lose them, and he declared that he would go in search of them, if he had to go alone. Old Blaze declared that he should not go alone, and volunteered to accompany him. It was settled, therefore, that the two men should go in search of the animals, and should join the others at the Devil's Gap, at which point they proposed to stop for a while.

Silverspur and Old Blaze set out in one direction, while their companions went in another. They followed the trail back to their last encampment, where they saw signs of the missing animals, but discovered that they had gone on without stopping. As it was useless to pursue them any further on foot, the two men encamped for the night among the trees that lined the banks of a creek.

In the morning they started to rejoin their comrades, and an accident befell them at the outset of the journey. Silverspur shot a deer before they proceeded far, and the animal fell to the ground, mortally wounded. Old Blaze, drawing his knife, ran to finish the deer, but stumbled and fell as he was running. As bad luck would have it, he fell upon his knife, which entered his thigh, making a deep and painful wound.

The gash was bound up immediately, and the hunter, after resting a little while, was able to walk, though his progress was slow and difficult.

Soon after this second start, Silverspur, happening to look around, discovered a large body of Indians, less than a quarter of a mile in their rear.

"What shall we do now?" he asked, as he pointed them out to his companion.

"What you kin do is plain enough," replied Blaze. "Yer legs are good, and you kin git away. As fur me, I can't run, and will hev to take my chances."

"Do you think I would leave you? You know me better than that, old man. I think we can both save ourselves. The Indians have seen us, no doubt, but have not found us out. They probably mistake us for some of their own people, as they are in no hurry to get to us. If you will pull up a little, until we get to the creek yonder, you can hide under the bank. The Indians will follow me, and you can get clear when they have gone by."

"Are you right sure, boy, that your legs are good?" asked the hunter, looking hard at his companion.

"I can trust them, and you need have no fear for me. The Indians are afoot, as you see, and I am sure that no runner among them can catch me before I reach the Devil's Gap."

"All right, then. Yer legs will hev to save yer own skelp and mine."

"Come on. I belive they are getting suspicions of us."

Old Blaze quickened his pace, and they soon reached the creek, where he concealed himself in the dense foliage under the bank.

Silverspur crossed the creek, and gained an elevation beyond it, from which he looked back at the Indians. They had become suspicious of the strangers, and runners from the main body were hastening toward the creek. As he started to run, the advanced Indians gave a yell, and pushed forward in pursuit.

The young man had not reckoned without his host, when he said that he could trust his legs. It was not their length that he confided in, but their activity and endurance. More than once they had served him well in grievous peril, and he had no doubt that they would carry him safely to his friends.

He halted but once—to see that the Indians did not stop at the creek to search for Old Blaze—before he had run a good two-mile stretch, and had put a considerable distance between himself and his pursuers. After that, he stopped whenever he found himself on a hill, to see whether they were gaining on him, half hoping that they might abandon the race. The hope was a vain one, as he well knew that Indian runners, when once started on a chase, will fall dead in their tracks, rather than give up the pursuit.

It was a long distance to the Devil's Gap, and Fred Wilder had not got his prairie legs on. He did not think of this when he proposed to draw the pursuit from his friend. If he had thought of it, it would not have prevented him from making the proposition. For a long time he had been leading the enervating life of a city, and his bodily powers were by no means such as they were when he left the mountains and the plains.

He was forced to confess to himself, when he stopped to look back, that he paused to gain breath, as much as to observe the progress of his pursuers. He was forced, also, to the unwelcome admission that they were gaining on him, slowly but surely.

He was growing weary—of that there could be no doubt. The summer day was hot; the sun shone scorchingly; there was no water on the route, and his throat was parched with thirst. Still his persevering and indefatigable pursuers gained on him, and their yells sounded horribly in his ears.

But it was past noon. He had run more than five hours, and he consoled himself with the thought that he must be near the rendezvous. He was willing that the Indians should gain on him a little, as they would soon be seen by his friends, and the tables would be turned on them so nicely!

It was with a sigh of relief, with a feeling of great joy, that he came within the shadow of the hills that marked the Gap. A few more steps, and he would be safe.

The few steps were taken, and he reached the encampment, only to find it deserted!

Silverspur was astounded by this appalling discovery. His head swam, and his body reeled. At that moment he felt so weak that exertion seemed impossible. His friends had gone up the river, and he could not guess how far. They might be a full day's journey in advance of him. How could he hope to overtake them, and to escape his fleet-footed pursuers.

In his despair, he thought only of satisfying his thirst. He was determined to drink, if he should die the next moment. He staggered down to the river, knelt at the brink, and drank as if he expected never to have another draught.

When he arose, the Indians were fearfully near him; but his strength and courage had returned. They had come upon the trail of the white men, and, fearing an ambuscade, had halted to reconnoiter. But for this circumstance, Silverspur would have been killed where he drank. As it was, he was in great danger, and their bullets and arrows whistled unpleasantly close to him as he mounted the bank. But he was rested and refreshed, his nerves were braced for a grand effort, and the consciousness of his peril gave him new energy and endurance.

He ran for his scalp, knowing that his possession of that precious part of his person depended on his speed. The Indians raised a yell as he shot ahead of them; but it was a feeble cry, compared to their previous shouts, and showed that their throats were dry and thirsty. They must stop to drink, and this thought gave him new hope. He resolved to make a long burst, hoping to get so far ahead of them that they would abandon the pursuit.

He was again mistaken. The savages stopped to quench their thirst; but they were resolved to overtake the fugitive or die on the trail. When he looked back, they were far in his rear, but were pressing determinedly on.

The young man knew that he had a long and hard race before him; but he believed that Providence would be propitious to a man that sacrificed himself for his friend. His hope was even brighter than it had been before he reached the rendezvous, and he felt that his will would supply him with strength.

On he pressed, through the long hours of the midsummer afternoon, with his red enemies straining after him. As he occasionally looked behind, he had the satisfaction of seeing that their line was gradually lengthened, and that one by one they dropped off, until but five continued the pursuit. But those five were gaining on him, and he felt that his strength was failing again.

Should he stop, and give battle to those five? He seriously considered the question, as that desperate chance seemed to be his only resource. No; the odds against him were too great, and he was so weak that he could hardly "count" in a hand-to-hand struggle.

"Let them screech," he said, as their exultant yells told him how confident they were of overtaking him. "They had better save their breath for running, or they may not catch me yet."

He toiled on, and until the sinking sun showed him that the day was near its close and until the number of his pursuers were diminished to three. His strength was nearly exhausted, his feet were so sore that every step was painful, and his legs had swollen until he seemed to drag them as a load. Thirst had overpowered him again; his throat was dry and hot; his breath came in difficult gasps; his head was dizzy and a mist floated before his eyes.

He could run no more. The end of the race had come and the only question was, how it should be ended. There were but three Indians now, and his rifle, which he had carried through the weary chase until its weight was no longer supportable, would do good work if his eye remained true. He might bring down one of his adversaries, and might load in time to shoot another, before they could close in upon him, and then he would have but one to deal with. It was his last chance, and he could do nothing but adopt it.

As he looked ahead, to find a suitable place to make a stand, he saw smoke rising from an elevation before him. The next moment he saw men on horseback. He pressed his hand before his eyes, as if to drive away the mist that blinded him, and he saw that they were white men.

They had perceived him, and they came galloping toward him. They were seen by the Indians, who turned and fled. The pursuers became the pursued, and small chance would they have in another race.

Silverspur saw nothing more. The mist closed in upon him thickly. His rifle fell upon the ground, and he dropped heavily beside it.

CHAPTER III.
THE GIRL WARRIOR.

Fred Wilder came to his senses as his friends were carrying him to their camp. They had gone on for the purpose of meeting a band of friendly Crows, supposing that Old Blaze and Silverspur would recover their horses, and would have no difficulty in overtaking them. When Silverspur told them of his adventure, and described his terrible race, he received plenty of sympathy, and praise from the open-hearted mountain men, who could well appreciate the motive that prompted him to incur such danger to save his friend.

"That was a purty smart run fur a chap from the settlements," said one of the party; "but it warn't a very big thing. I've knowed Indian runners to make more than a hundred miles in a day."

It was a big enough thing to suit Silverspur, and his swelled legs were somewhat too big to please him. He was in such pain that he was hardly able to stir for several days. Fortunately for him he was not obliged to move. His companions had encamped with a band of Crows, and expected to remain a week or longer in that locality.

The men who had gone in pursuit of Silverspur's pursuers brought in three scalps, and declared that the runners were Arapahoes. Bad Eye, the chief of the Crows, said that they might expect an attack, as the Arapahoes were probably awaiting an opportunity to pounce upon his people, toward whom they had lately manifested the most inveterate hostility.

The third day after Silverspur's arrival, Old Blaze came limping into the camp, and was overjoyed at finding his friend alive. The Indians had passed within a few feet of him without observing him. When they had gone by he crawled out of his hiding-place, and followed the trail as rapidly as he could, being compelled to seek concealment every now and then, to avoid straggling parties of Indians.

He brought the intelligence that the Arapahoes were a war-party, that they were in strong force, and that they were undoubtedly intending to commit depredations upon the Crows. As this coincided with the opinion of Bad Eye, the camp was removed to a bend in the river, and the Indians, with their white allies, began to fortify the position. A slight breastwork was thrown up across the bend, and the horses were driven back into the semicircle, as the rear of the camp was rendered impregnable by the river.

The next morning the Arapahoes came in sight, and the camp was fairly invested. The Crows and the white men, perceiving that they were largely outnumbered, made every preparation for defense.

The Arapahoes seemed inspired by a desperate resolution to exterminate the band of Crows. They made charge after charge upon the breastwork, with the greatest fury, and on two occasions nearly gained possession of it. The white men persuaded their Indian allies to act altogether upon the defensive, to content themselves with repulsing the attacks of their assailants, and to labor as much as possible to strengthen their position. By this means, they argued, the Arapahoes would tire themselves out, and, when they should become wearied, they might be charged and put to flight.

Night put a stop to the struggle, and the Crows hoped that their inveterate enemies would retire from the contest; but in this they were mistaken. In the morning the assault was vigorously renewed, and it was only by the most determined fighting that the Crows could hold their ground. If it had not been for the assistance of the white men, they must have been driven into the river, and nearly all of them would have perished.

By noon the attack had slackened considerably. It became evident that the ranks of the Arapahoes had been thinned by the close fire of their antagonists, and that they had become fatigued by the incessant labor of battle. The time had come for the besieged to assume the offensive, and they prepared to attack in their turn. Old Blaze gave directions for horses to be made ready for fifty men, with whom he proposed to make a détour through the timber, and fall upon the rear of the enemy, while the others should charge in front.

Foremost among the Arapahoes, urging them on in every attack, and fearlessly leading the charge up to the very muzzles of their guns at the breastwork, was a person who attracted attention from the beginning of the engagement, and who was soon recognized as a woman. The Crow chief said that she was the same woman who had been conspicuous in several attacks upon the Crows, and Old Blaze, believing her to be the person of whom White Shield had spoken, told Silverspur that Dove-eye was among the combatants.

Fred Wilder was so weak and sore after his hard race, that he was unable to take part in the battle; but, when he learned that Dove-eye was in the ranks of the Arapahoes, he could not restrain his impatience to see her.

Without speaking of his intention to Old Blaze, who would not have allowed him to move, he crawled out of the lodge in which he had been lying, saddled a horse, mounted, and rode forward to the breastwork, where the Crows were preparing to charge upon their adversaries.

The charge was made before he reached the forest. The Arapahoes discovered, as they began to fall from their horses, that they were attacked in the rear, and were thrown into confusion. The Crows and their white allies took advantage of this moment to sally out and fall upon their foes. As they were comparatively fresh, both men and horses, while the Arapahoes were wearied by their repeated assaults, the movement was a complete success.

Silverspur, hardly able to sit on his horse, soon perceived that it would be useless for him to attempt to overtake the charging party, and he took his station upon an eminence, from which he could have a good view of the surrounding country.

He saw that the Arapahoes were already broken, and were flying in all directions, hotly pursued by their vindictive antagonists. He looked in every quarter for Dove-eye; but his head was so dizzy, and his eyes were so dim, that he was unable to see far, and he was about to move away, when a warrior came galloping up the slope toward him. As the warrior approached, he perceived that it was a woman. A moment more, and he recognized Dove-eye.

She was beautiful indeed. Silverspur thought that he had never seen any wild thing that was half so lovely, and it did not detract from her beauty and grace that she was riding man-fashion, as a warrior must. She was richly attired in the Indian style; her head was crowned with a plume of painted feathers, and her saddle was a panther's skin. She rode a splendid coal-black horse, and carried a battle-ax in her right hand. Her hair, unlike the coarse and straight locks of the rest of her tribe, was wavy and inclined to curl; her complexion was a rich olive, instead of copper-color, and she had not the high cheek-bones peculiar to the Indian race. With her cheeks guiltless of paint, glowing with excitement, and her eyes flashing fire, she was beautiful indeed.

Silverspur urged his horse toward her as she rode up the slope, and called her by name; but she whirled her battle-ax in the air, and launched it full at his head. As he dodged to avoid the missile his small remnant of strength deserted him, and he fell from his horse to the ground. When he recovered himself, the warrior was out of hearing.

Picking up the battle-ax, he slowly walked back up to camp, whither his horse had preceded him.

The Crows came in loaded with scalps and full of joy. Although they had lost a number of warriors, they had a grand scalp-dance, in which the women participated most heartily. Silverspur and Old Blaze did not join the dance, but conversed of Dove-eye and of her part in the battle.

"She fit like a tiger," said the trapper. "It's my opeenyun that she's got a partic'lar spite ag'inst the Crows, judgin' by the way she pitched into 'em."

"It is sad to think that she should have taken up the battle-ax and become so bloodthirsty."

"Rayther sad fur the Crows, shore enough. Her lettin' go the battle-ax would hev been sadder fur you, ef ye hadn't dodged the weapon. Are you sartin it is the same gal?"

"I have not a doubt of it. I saw her plainly, and I could not be mistaken. Those flashing eyes, that rich olive complexion, that queenly carriage, could not be forgotten. There was no change in her, except that she seemed more beautiful than ever."

"Yaas, I reckon. Handsome is as handsome does, 'cordin' to my notion, and it don't look over and above handsome to see a gal trottin' out on the war-path and flingin' bloody battle-axes about. 'Pears like she didn't know ye."

"I suppose she did not," replied Wilder, as his countenance fell.

"A knock-down blow with that battle-ax of her'n wouldn't be what ye might call a love-tap, and it warn't no common way of lettin' ye know that she hadn't forgot ye. But ye oughtn't to be down-hearted, boy. Remember how ye fooled Old Blaze down to St. Louey. Tell ye, thar's a powerful differ atween a chap with long ha'r and beard, and his face brown and his leggin's on, and the same chap when he is short-sheared and class-shaved, and has got the look of the settlements onto him. The gal was just from the fight, too, whar every white man was an inimy. Ye may count it sartin that she didn't know ye."

"I believe you are right. I must find her, old friend."

"I allowed ye'd found her to-day. Leastways, ye found her battle-ax."

"I must see her and speak to her. If it is necessary to go among the Arapahoes to find her, I must seek her there. Will you help me, or is it too much to ask?"

"Ye kin bet yer life that Old Blaze will stand by ye."

CHAPTER IV.
THE PROPHET'S CHILD

A wild place among the hills, on the eastern slope of the Rocky Mountains. At the base of a cliff is a rude hut, forming the entrance to a cave in the rock. A plateau before the cliff commands a view of broken hills and ravines, becoming less rugged as they descend and finally melting into the wide expanse of prairie that stretches endlessly toward the east.

Among these hills and ravines a fearful scene is being acted. A party of Arapaho Indians have been surprised by a band of Crows, who have attacked them with such vigor that they are flying in all directions, pursued by their bloodthirsty and vindictive adversaries. The air resounds with shouts and yells, with screams and shrieks; blood is scattered plentifully upon the hills, and the ravines are filled with horror.

From the plateau in front of the hut two persons are gazing at the terrible sight below them. One is an old Indian with bent form and white hair. A blanket is wrapped around him, and his countenance expresses the deepest distress. The other is a girl of the same tribe, tall and graceful, much lighter in color than the Arapahoes, with long and wavy hair, and with beautiful features. She stands as if spell-bound, and watches the carnage with eyes full of fear and anxiety.

"Come, my child," said the old man. "Our enemies are victorious, and we must fly."

"Is it really you, my father?" she asked, turning upon him with a look of wonder. "I thought you had gone to the spirit-land."

"I had; but my people were in danger, and I returned."

"Can you do nothing to help them? Many of them have been killed, and the rest are flying in all directions. What Indians are those who are pursuing them?"

"They are Crows. See, Dove-eye; they are coming up the hill toward us. We shall be killed if we remain here. Come; we must seek a hiding-place."

Seizing the girl by the hand, he hurried her along the plateau, to a rift that led up into the mountain. This they ascended with difficulty, until they reached another level space, covered with clumps of pine and cedar.

"Remain here, my child," said the old man as he led her into the cover of the trees. "I must go and see what becomes of our people, and what the Crows are doing. Do not stir until I return."

He was absent fully half an hour, during which time Dove-eye was filled with anxiety. Her friends the Arapahoes were being slaughtered by their merciless foes, and she could still hear from her elevated position the yells and shrieks of the victors and the vanquished. But this was not all. There was a white man below whom she had saved from death at the hands of the Arapahoes, and toward whom her feelings were such as had never before been excited in her breast. She had concealed him in a hole in the cliff and he was lying there, wounded and helpless, an easy prey to any foe who should discover his hiding-place.

When the old man returned, he was greatly excited, and was trembling from fear and exhaustion.

"Come, my child," he said. "We are not safe here. We must seek another hiding-place. We must go up further into the mountains."

"Sit down and rest yourself," replied Dove-eye. "We can not be seen here. You are so tired that you can hardly stand."

"There is no time for rest. The Crows are everywhere in the hills, searching for our friends who have escaped them. If they see our trail, we will soon be discovered."

"Where is the white man? Where is Silverspur? I am afraid that they may find him and kill him."

"They have already found him, and he is dead."

"Dead! Are you sure, my father?"

"I saw him dragged out and struck down with a tomahawk."

"Were they Crows who killed him, or Arapahoes?"

"They were Crows."

The girl was a picture of despair. She sat still, as if she had been turned into stone, gazing into vacancy. Then her cheeks flushed, and a wild and fierce light blazed in her dark eyes. The fires of hatred and vengeance had been kindled in her breast.

"I must see him, my father," she said, quietly. "Perhaps he is only wounded."

"Do you think the Crows would leave him alive? I tell you he is dead."

"I must see him."

"The Crows would kill you, also."

"I am not afraid of the Crows. If he is dead, they will let me bury him."

"Has the mind of Dove-eye been taken from her? If the Crows should not kill you, they would carry you away, and I would never see you again. You promised me, Dove-eye, if I would save the life of the white man, that you would never leave me while I lived."

"It is true, my father; but he is dead."

"I saved his life, as I promised to do. He was not killed by the Arapahoes, but by the Crows."

"The word of Dove-eye is sacred. I will go with you."

The old man and the girl sought and found a refuge further up the mountain from the search of the pursuing Crows. They came down, in a nearly famished condition, when the scattered Arapahoes returned; but they did not remain long in that locality, as the remnant of the band to which they were attached removed toward the south. After the expiration of several months they came back to the scene of their disastrous defeat, and Dove-eye and the old man again occupied the lodge at the foot of the cliff.

The girl passed her time in mourning the loss of the white man who had become so dear to her. This occupation caused her to grow thin and pale, and might have caused her death, if she had not been diverted from it by another trouble. The old man, who had never recovered from the effects of his fright and exhaustion at the time of the attack of the Crows, sickened and died.

Dove-eye, who had known him as a great medicine man, whose influence in his tribe was almost unbounded, was puzzled as well as grieved, when she saw him lying there, pale and cold, with glassy eyes, hollow cheeks and dropped under-jaw, to all appearance a corpse.

He had been subject to trances—had been in the habit of falling into a sleep which, whether real or counterfeit, closely resembled death. He knew when these spells were coming on, and it had been his custom to notify the tribe that on such an occasion, at a certain hour in the morning, he would go to the spirit-land, and that he would return at noon. The warriors would solemnly come to visit him and look upon him as he lay in this trance, satisfying themselves that he was really dead. After noon they would again come, when they would find him alive, and would listen to the messages which he had brought from the other world. By this mysterious power the old man maintained his ascendancy over the tribe. His word was law, and his advice was always heeded.

It was possible, Dove-eye thought, that he might then be on one of his journeys to the spirit-world. He had sent no announcement of his intentions to the tribe; but he might have forgotten to do so. She said nothing, but waited to see whether he would rise at his usual hour. Noon came, and he remained motionless and cold. The evening passed, and night came on, without bringing any change. The next morning there was no alteration in him, except for the worse, and Dove-eye was convinced that he was dead.

She then felt that she had sustained a great loss, and thought seriously about her future. If the old man had not adopted her, and retained her as his companion, she would have been compelled to share the lodge of some warrior, with one or two other squaws. Now that her protector was gone she would be sought by many, and would be unable to resist their importunities.

In her desperation she hit upon an expedient, which, if it should prove successful, would enable her to retain her independence, and would gratify the vengeance that had so long slumbered in her heart.

A negro slave of the tribe named Jose, who had been captured in Texas or Mexico, had long been the servant of the medicine-man, and was devoted to Dove-eye. With his assistance she buried the body of the old man, swearing him to secrecy concerning the burial.

She then went to the village, and called together the old men, whom she informed that their Big Medicine had gone to the spirit-land, and that he would return when six moons had passed.

This announcement filled them with surprise and sorrow; but their credulity was not shaken. Dove-eye had often brought them messages from the old man, and they were prepared to believe whatever she might say.

She went on to tell them that the Great Spirit was angry with them because they had not punished the Crows for their unprovoked attack, by which so many Arapahoes had been slain. The old man had advised them to go on the war-path against the Crows, and to continue fighting them until ample vengeance should be taken for that massacre. He had also commanded her to assume the garb and weapons of a warrior, and to accompany all expeditions that should be sent against the Crows.

Dove-eye waited with great anxiety to learn what would be the effect of her communication. It was received in silence, and she was ordered to retire until the old men should have deliberated over it. After the lapse of an hour she was admitted to the council-lodge, and Black Horse, the head chief, acquainted her with the result of the deliberation.

"It is well," he said. "The Big Medicine has left us, to be gone a long time, and our hearts are sad. Never before, when he has gone to the spirit-land, has he remained so long away from his people. But we are not lost without him; for he has sent us a message, and has left us advice. His words have always been good words, and Dove-eye has never lied to us. We will go upon the war-path against the Crows, and Dove-eye shall be among the warriors. The young men must not look upon her."

The season of mourning followed, for the old medicine-man, who was believed to be dead for the space of six moons, and then the whole strength of the tribe was employed in expeditions against the Crows. Dove-eye, arrayed and armed as a brave, was an honored member of every war-party, and acted her part with such skill and bravery as to command the approval of the whole tribe. When the braves rehearsed their exploits, she was always allowed to tell her own, and her achievements did not fall far behind those of the most renowned warriors. With every blow she struck, she believed that she was avenging the death of Silverspur.

CHAPTER V.
THE SNAKE.

It had been the hope and expectation of Dove-eye that she would be killed in battle, or that something would occur to release her from her obligations, before the time appointed for the return of the old medicine-man. But the six months passed away, and found her still living and the Indians joyfully expectant of a visit from their beloved prophet.

Thus far her plan had succeeded admirably; but, if her imposition should be discovered, she knew that a fearful death awaited her. Providence had not interfered in her behalf, and she saw no way to avert the calamity.

Not knowing what to do, Dove-eye did nothing. She did not fully realize the necessity of coming to some decision in the matter, until she was summoned to the presence of the head chief.

"Has the tongue of Dove-eye become crooked?" inquired Black Horse. "Did the pale-face girl who was in her lodge last summer teach her to tell lies? Has the Big Medicine gone to the spirit-land, never to return, or shall we see him again?"

"How shall I know more than the chief knows?"

"Dove-eye told us that he would return after six moons; but six moons have passed, and we have not seen him."

"Have six moons passed?" asked the girl, with a look of surprise. "Is the chief sure of this?"

"I am sure. My people are tired of waiting for him. We have done as he told us to do. We have fought the Crows, and have gained many victories. We have taken a great revenge for the cruel attack they made upon us. But we are weary of war, and we have lost many young men. We wish to rest, to rebuild our lodges, and to gather skins to sell to the traders. Why does not the Big Medicine return to us?"

"Perhaps," suggested Dove-eye, at a loss for an excuse, "they do not count time in the spirit-land as we count it here. Perhaps The Big Medicine has returned. It is several suns since I have visited the lodge at the cliff. If the chief will permit me, I will go there now, and will watch for the Big Medicine, if he is not already there. As he promised to return, he will surely do so."

The consent of the chief was given, and Dove-eye, dressing herself in woman's attire, took up her residence in the lodge at the foot of the cliff.

This was for the purpose of gaining time, in order that she might reflect upon the matter, and determine what course she had best pursue.

At the end of four days she came to the village, and informed Black Horse that she had a message for him. The old men were convened in the council-lodge, where she was brought before them, and was ordered to declare her errand.

She said that she had seen the Big Medicine, who had been well received in the spirit-land, and who had met there many of the warriors who had been slain in recent encounters. She mentioned the names of those whom he had met and described their pursuits in the happy hunting-grounds, and the honors that were bestowed upon them. This part of her subject she treated with consummate tact, knowing how to adopt the style of the old man, and how to flatter the vanity of her auditors. She succeeded so well, that the Arapahoes were highly pleased, and considered themselves favored above all other men, in receiving such consoling messages from the other world.

She went on to say that the Great Spirit was highly pleased with the punishment which they had inflicted upon the Crows; but the warriors who had been killed in battle still demanded vengeance. The Big Medicine advised them to persist in their enmity to the Crows, and to strike them whenever an opportunity offered, although they need not entirely abandon the pursuits of peace for the purpose of engaging in war.

At this there were visible signs of disapproval among the old men; but Dove-eye, nothing daunted, went on to declare the last and the worst of her errand.

The Big Medicine, she said, had been suffered to leave the spirit-land but for a short time, and had not been permitted to visit his people; but he would return to them after the lapse of six more moons, and would never again leave them, until he should be finally taken away. He exhorted them to give themselves no uneasiness concerning him, as his absence was for their good, and he was continually watching over them and guiding them. It was his last request that Dove-eye should again be allowed to assume the garb and weapons of a warrior.

The old men received this portion of the message in the most profound silence; but Dove-eye could not fail to see that their displeasure was great. For this she cared little, as she had taken the risk, and was not afraid of their frowns. If her secret should be discovered, she knew that death was certain, and her only chance was to continue the imposture.

No direct action was taken upon Dove-eye's second communication; but the message was tacitly heeded. The warfare against the Crows was kept up in a desultory manner, and the presence of the girl, when she joined the war-parties, was not objected to. Still, she saw that there were those who looked upon her with suspicion, and she hoped that an honorable death in battle might put an end to her troubles, and absolve her from all liability.

There was a white trader residing among the Arapahoes at this time, named Silas Wormley, a cunning, foxy man, shrewd enough at driving a small bargain, but incapable of any enterprise that demanded enlarged ideas. He had gained the favor of the tribe by procuring supplies for them when they were short of peltries to give in exchange. This accommodation had greatly pleased them, as they had not troubled themselves to think of the exorbitant prices which they were to pay in the future.

Silas Wormley had come among the Arapahoes shortly after Dove-eye had joined the warriors. The warfare in which they were engaged was very distasteful to him, as it interfered seriously with his anticipated profits. While the Indians were fighting, death was depriving him of the opportunity of collecting some of his debts, and those who lived were not engaged in such pursuits as would enable them to pay what they owed.

When he heard the story of the visits of the Big Medicine to the spirit-land, he laughed inwardly at the credulity of the Indians, although he knew better than to offend them by ridiculing their pet belief. The second communication of Dove-eye made him highly indignant. He knew that she was an impostor, but could not guess whether she was aided in her imposture by the old medicine-man, who might still be living and deceiving the Indians for some purpose of his own. However that might be, Dove-eye was an impostor, and ought to be exposed and punished.

But Silas Wormley had no thought of exposing and punishing her. A better, or worse, feeling had been stirred up in his breast, and he had become, after his fashion, violently enamored of Dove-eye. He was determined to possess her, by some means and in some manner. He had asked her of Black Horse for a wife, but had been informed that she was a warrior, by command of the Big Medicine, and as such could not be given in marriage. He had, also, been well laughed at by the young braves who had in vain endeavored to induce Dove-eye to enter their lodges.

When Dove-eye, by her second revelation from the spirit-land, had extended her privilege as a warrior, Wormley was decidedly of the opinion that she was going entirely too far, and that a stop should be put to the imposture. Knowing that she must have been imposing upon the Indians, he thought that it would not be difficult for him to obtain proof of the fact. Then he could threaten her with exposure, and thus compel her to accede to his wishes.

With this view he waylaid her, for the purpose of speaking privately with her, and met her as she was walking alone in the forest.

It may as well be mentioned here, that the Arapahoes, recognizing the craft and duplicity of Wormley, had named him the Snake. It was really, in their estimation, a title of honor, and the trader did not care by what name he was called, as long as it did not interfere with his plans of profit.

"How long," he asked, after a little preliminary conversation, "does Dove-eye suppose that she can deceive her people?"

The girl, who had been meditating upon her imposture, was startled by this abrupt inquiry, and turned upon him with a look of surprise, mingled with alarm.

"The words of the Snake are strange words," she said, recovering her composure. "What does he mean?"

"You know well enough what I mean. You know that you have been deceiving the Arapahoes for a long time, by representing to them that the Big Medicine has gone to the spirit-land. These Indians don't know any better than to believe such nonsense; but I have known, all the time, that you have been deceiving them."

"The tongue of the Snake is forked. He speaks falsely when he says that the Big Medicine has not gone to the spirit-land. Dove-eye has spoken the truth."

"Tush, girl! You need not think that you can carry it off with me in that way. Don't I know that he is alive, and that you have concealed him from the tribe?"

"How can you know that which is not true?" replied Dove-eye, with a look of triumph. "I swear before the Great Spirit, that I have not concealed the Big Medicine."

"I was only joking with you," said Wormley, perceiving that he had made a mistake, and had got on the "wrong tack." "I wished to convince you that I know what you really have done. It is true that the Big Medicine has gone to the spirit-land; but it is also true that he will never return. He is dead, and you have buried him."

This was a home thrust, and it brought the blood to the cheeks of the troubled girl.

"He is dead," continued the trader, "and you are deceiving the people to serve your own purpose, because you are not willing to marry; but you can't fool me. You want to get the same influence over the tribe that the old man had; but I know that his trips to the spirit-land were nothing but nonsense, and that the messages which you pretend to bring from him have not a word of truth in them."

"You had better tell the warriors," suggested Dove-eye, "that the Big Medicine is a liar, and that he has always deceived them."

"You can't scare me in that way, girl. Of course I am not fool enough to tell the Arapahoes that I don't believe that nonsense; but I mean to let you know that you are found out. The old men suspect that you have been cheating them. What do you suppose they would do to you, if I should tell them the truth of the matter?"

"If you should tell them lies, they would take your scalp."

"But you know that it would not be a lie, and you would be cut in pieces. I tell you, Dove-eye, that your life is in my hands. If I expose you, you will surely be killed. If I do not expose you, you must be found out before long. I can save you. I can arrange matters so that this deception will never be discovered. I only ask you to be my wife, and all will be well."

Instead of answering him, Dove-eye gave him a scornful glance, and turned away and left him.

CHAPTER VI.
CONFESSION UNDER TORTURE.

Silas Wormley was pretty sure of the ground he trod on, but was not absolutely certain. Although the manner of Dove-eye had convinced him that he had guessed the truth, or very near it, he felt that he was not able to prove his assertions. If he should charge her with the deception, before the old men of the Arapahoes, he knew that their own suspicions would not be strong enough to confirm his accusations. They would require plain and undeniable proof to convince them of the falsity of that which they had so long held as a religious belief. If he should fail in furnishing such proof, he would lose the profits of his trading, if not his scalp.

He determined, therefore, to make his suspicion a certainty, and he was not long in forming a plan to accomplish that end.

He knew that Jose, the negro, had long been the servant and constant companion of the old medicine-man, and that he was devoted to Dove-eye. It was not to be supposed that the old man could have died without the knowledge of Jose, and it was probable that he had assisted Dove-eye in disposing of the body. Wormley had seen enough of the negro to know that he could not be bribed from his duty to Dove-eye, and that the secret, if he really knew it, must be forced from him.

To accomplish this, a confederate was necessary, and the trader cast about for a suitable person.

There was an Indian among the Arapahoes, supposed to be a Pawnee Loup by birth, who never joined a war party, and who had no belongings of any kind, not even a gun or a squaw or a lodge. This individual, who was known by the name of Bull-tail, was an ill-conditioned vagabond, the butt of the village, and the general recipient of all scattering kicks and cuffs.

The trader bribed Bull-tail, by the promise of some rum, to assist him in his undertaking, and the two came upon Jose and seized him, one morning when he was away from his lodge.

"I have got an account to settle with you, boy," said the trader. "I am going to ask you a question, and you had better tell the truth, or I will squeeze it out of you the hard way. Where did you and Dove-eye bury the Big Medicine?"

The countenance of the negro, at this unexpected question, convinced Wormley that he had hit the mark, and he proceeded to press his advantage.

"You needn't try to lie out of it," he said, "or to get out of it in any way; for I know pretty near all about the matter. Dove-eye has admitted to me that the old man died, and that you helped her bury him, and I only want you to show me where the grave is."

The name of Dove-eye brought the negro to his senses. He perceived that, whatever she might have admitted, she had not revealed the place of burial of the old man, and he was determined to disclose nothing that she had not been willing to make known. He stoutly denied all knowledge of the grave, or of the death of the old man, or of any thing connected with his disappearance.

"Very well," said the trader. "I know that you are lying, and I have advised you to tell the truth. If you don't tell it, I must squeeze it out of you."

As the negro persisted in refusing to make any disclosures, he was gagged, stripped, and tied to a tree. The trader cut hickory rods, which he plied upon the back of the poor fellow until he was tired of the exercise, and then turned over the task to Bull-tail, who, having received several flagellations, thought it a great privilege to be permitted to whip somebody.

Jose kicked and writhed and groaned in his agony; but, when the gag was removed from his mouth, he refused to utter a word.

"I'll have it out of you yet!" exclaimed Wormley, with an oath. "In the settlements, when we get hold of a tough customer, and he won't let the truth come out of him, we choke it out, and that's the way I will serve you, you black rascal!"

He had brought a rope, which he knotted in the most approved style, and placed around Jose's neck, throwing the loose end over the limb of a tree. After exhorting the negro to confess, Wormley and the Indian hauled him up until his feet were off the ground, but soon lowered him.

"You see what it is, boy," said the trader. "You had better make up your mind to show us that grave, or you will get a choking ten times worse than this."

As the negro persisted in his denial, notwithstanding this rough treatment, Wormley ran him up again, and angrily took a turn with the rope around a sapling.

The agony of Jose was fearful, and was increased by his struggles. His eyes rolled back in his head, his tongue protruded from his mouth, and then he was quiet.

Fearing that he had been killed, the trader let him down. He was senseless when the rope was removed from his neck; but a liberal application of cold water brought him to after a while, and he sat up and stared helplessly about.

"Have I been dead?" he asked.

"Mighty near it, boy," replied Wormley. "If you ain't willing, now, to show us where you and Dove-eye buried the Big Medicine, you will go up again, and then you will never come down."

Jose's pluck and determination had oozed out of him, under the last trial, and he signified his willingness to show them the place, if they would allow him to rest a few minutes and regain his strength.

This request was granted, and he led them to the ravine in which the old man was buried. Wormley sharpened a stick, and dug up the ground, making the Indian and the negro throw out the earth with their hands, until the body was partially uncovered. In spite of decomposition, Bull-tail recognized the features of the Big Medicine, as well as his long white hair and beard and the peculiar robe that he had always worn.

Having satisfied himself, the trader replaced the earth, and permitted Jose to depart, after warning him not to mention to Dove-eye the treatment he had received, or the disclosure he had made.

Jose heeded the warning until he was out of sight of Wormley, when he hastened to find Dove-eye, and tell her all that happened.

She was greatly troubled. Discovery seemed imminent, if not unavoidable, and a terrible death stared her in the face. The negro was very indignant at learning that Wormley had lied to him concerning the admissions which she was said to have made, and he forgot his own pain at the sight of the anxiety of his young mistress.

Accusing himself of having brought this trouble upon her, he resolved to endeavor to extricate her from her embarrassment and at the same time to make Wormley repent of the base part he was playing. At first he wished to kill the trader; but Dove-eye said his death would avail nothing, as long as Bull-tail was also possessed of the secret. He then suggested flight; but Dove-eye declared that she might as well die there, as to starve in the mountains, or to be captured by some other tribe.

At last he hit upon an idea that pleased him amazingly, and he burst into a laugh as it came into his mind. Bidding his mistress set her mind at rest, he hastened to carry out his plan.

Removing the earth from the grave in the ravine, he carried away the remains of the old medicine-man, and buried them in another spot. He then took up the body of an Indian who had been buried so long that his features could not be recognized, and laid it in the grave, filling in the earth so that it looked exactly as Wormley had left it.

Having finished his task, he hastened to Dove-eye, and told her what he had done.

Dove-eye was overjoyed. She praised the negro highly for the ready wit and invention by which he had extricated her from this pressing peril, and declared that the Snake might do his worst, as she was not afraid of him, and was able to turn the tables upon him whenever he should seek to harm her.

The trader, satisfied that he had Dove-eye in his power, lost no time in pressing his advantage. Cautioning Bull-tail to say nothing about the discovery that had been made, he sought an opportunity of speaking to Dove-eye privately. She did not avoid him, as she was by no means unwilling to have the affair brought "to a head."

"Dove-eye will listen to me now," he said. "She must listen to me, unless she is willing to die. I knew that I was right when I told her that she was deceiving her people; but I was not then able to prove my words. Now I have the proof, and Dove-eye is in my power. She must do as I wish her to do, or I will denounce her to the old men."

"What will you do?" calmly asked Dove-eye. "You had better not tell the warriors that the Big Medicine has lied to them."

"I will tell them that you have deceived them. I will tell them that the Big Medicine will never return from the spirit-land, that he is dead and in his grave."

"It is easy for the Snake to tell lies."

"I can prove that I speak the truth. I will take them to his grave, and will show them his body."

"It will be hard even for the Snake to show that which is not to be found."

"But I have seen it. You thought your secret was safe with you and Jose; but he has confessed, and has shown me where you buried the old man."

"You may be able to make Jose say many things; but he could not show you that which he has never seen himself."

"I have seen the body of the Big Medicine, and I can take the old men to his grave, where they can see it themselves. I wish to save you, Dove-eye. I wish you to live and to be my wife. If you will marry me, you will be safe; if not, I will tell the tribe of what you have done."

"If all you say were true, I had rather die than become your wife; but I am not afraid of your lies."

With this reply the girl turned away and left him.

Boiling with indignation at the contempt with which he was treated, the trader hastened to the village, and went at once to the lodge of Black Horse, whom he requested to call together the old men as he had a matter of the greatest importance to communicate.

The chief summoned the council, the door of the council-lodge was closed, and Wormley was about to commence his accusation, when he was interrupted by an uproar without.

CHAPTER VII.
OLD BLAZE IN A TIGHT PLACE.

"Durn the bushes!"

It was Old Blaze who spoke. He was slowly working his way through a thicket, in pitchy darkness, and at every step he either stumbled against a stone, or was brushed in the face by the limbs of the scraggy saplings that abounded in the place.

"Durn the bushes! 'Pears like I won't never git nowhar to-night. The dark comes down in chunks, and e'en a'most smothers me, and these hyar bushes are the peskiest things I ever lit into."

Thus muttering and grumbling, the hunter pushed on, until he was fairly out of the thicket.

"I reckon it's all plain sailin' now," said he. "But it's darker out in the open than 'twas in thar, or this ole hoss has gone clean blind. Hello! what's this?"

"This" was a perpendicular wall of rock, against which he had walked in the darkness.

"I 'lowed it was a thicker chunk of dark than or'nary," he muttered, "that had come along and struck me; but it seems to be solid rock. Wonder, now, ef this hyar ain't the very place whar Silverspur tumbled over and nearly killed hisself. I wish I'd let the boy come on this chase, as he wanted to, 'stead of leavin' him up thar in the hills; but I shouldn't wonder ef he gits the wind of the game afore I do, arter all. Wal, this rock cain't be stepped over, and I reckon I'd best camp right hyar and wait till mornin'."

Without further ceremony, he laid down at the foot of the cliff, and was soon sound asleep.

In the morning he was awake at the first glimpse of day, examined the position in which he had passed the night, and reached, by a *détour* that avoided the cliff, the high ground above. Before him was a bit of prairie, and beyond the prairie was a broad belt of woodland. He crossed the prairie, and entered the timber, moving cautiously, as he knew that the Indian village he was seeking could not be far off.

From the edge of the belt of trees he saw the lodges, on the wooded plain before him, and red-men and women walking about among them.

"This is all correct, as fur as heerd from," he muttered; "but thar's suthin' wrong somewhar. 'Pears to me that I smell Injuns, and the critturs are up to some devilment, or Old Blaze is mighty bad fooled. Thar's one of 'em, and thar's another! By the livin' possums of old Varginny! the timber's full of 'em!"

He had turned, and he saw that the forest which he had just traversed was alive with Indians. They had discovered his approach, had glided into his rear unobserved, and were closing in upon him. As soon as he saw them, they raised a yell, and rushed forward to capture him.

His quick glance told him that he was surrounded on all sides, except that toward the village. Blaming himself for the lack of caution that had led him into the hornets' nest, he saw that he had no time to lose, and made up his mind in an instant. He must run for his life, and he would hardly save it by running in the direction in which his foes were awaiting him. He must go where they were not expecting him, and that course led directly through the village.

As the yells of the Indians rose behind him, he answered them with a whoop, and bounded away toward the village. It was situated about two hundred yards from his starting point, and the route lay across a level plain, where scattered trees afforded him a partial cover.

Bullets and arrows whistled and sung about him as he ran; but he did not heed them; his attention was concentrated upon the task before him, and he did not fear the foe in his rear.

The Indians at the village, not expecting that his flight would take such a direction, knew nothing of the presence of the fugitive, until he burst in among them, dodging behind the lodges, and performing many strange antics, as he twisted and turned, to avoid the missiles of his pursuers. Then the women screamed, and the men yelled and ran for their weapons, joining the chase.

But Old Blaze had safely passed through the village, and it is probable that he would have succeeded in distancing his pursuers, had it not been for the peculiar nature of the country in which he found himself.

The Indians, knowing what must shortly happen, sent a strong force of well-armed runners to the left. The hunter soon found his course stopped by a deep chasm that lay in front and to the right of him. The chasm was impassable, and the only avenue of escape was at the left; but this was blocked up, as he quickly perceived, by a body of his enemies, who were also closing in behind him.

Under these circumstances, Old Blaze concluded that it would be better for him to surrender, than to exasperate the Indians by fighting to the death.

He threw down his rifle and tomahawk, and advanced toward his pursuers, holding out his hand, with a ludicrous attempt at a smile.

"As ye seem to want me so bad, red-skins, I'll come to ye," he said: "but it's a-treatin' a feller mighty rough, when he comes a-visitin' of ye, to chase him as if he was a varmint."

The Indians made no reply to this speech, but quietly bound their captive, and carried him to the village, where he was tied to a stake near the council-lodge.

It was an unpleasant predicament in which Old Blaze found himself; but he was not one of those men who despair. While life lasted, there was a chance to escape; if death should come, he would meet it like a man. It was not long before he had reason to hope.

He saw a white man passing through the village. Although attired in the Indian fashion, this man was undoubtedly white. He might be a renegade, who had become a savage in nature, as well as in dress; or he might be a trader, who would assent to every thing the Indians chose to do, for the sake of gaining their favor. At all events, his face was white, and he could not entirely have lost sympathy with the race from which he sprung.

The prisoner beckoned to him; but Silas Wormley (for he was the white man) did not appear to notice the signal. On the contrary, he quickened his pace, as if he was desirous of "passing by on the other side." But, when he was called upon in the English language, in tones that plainly showed that he was known to be a white man, he was obliged to stop and turn around, with a look of affected surprise. He slowly walked over to where the captive was standing, and was accosted by Old Blaze rather roughly, considering the fact that the hunter needed his assistance.

"I say, stranger, has anybody sent fur ye, in a big hurry?"

"No. What do you mean by that?"

"Didn't scare ye bad—did I?—when I made signals to ye from over hyar?"

"As I saw no signals, it is not to be supposed that I was to be scared by them."

"Kinder short-sighted, p'r'aps. When a man gits to lookin' at dollars right hard, 'pears like he cain't see nothin' else. Ye don't say whether ye're glad to see me, or not."

"I am truly sorry to see you here as a prisoner, although your manner is not calculated to excite sympathy."

"Old Blaze ain't much of a calkilation' man, I'm afeard."

"I heard that a prisoner had been taken, but supposed it to be an Indian. You are a white man, I believe."

"Did ye raally hear that thar rumpus? I'm glad to know that ye ain't quite so hard o' hearin' as mought hev been expected. I do allow that I'm a white man, stranger—white all over. Are you fixed up that way?"

"It is a strange question to ask. You see that I am a white man."

"Are ye on good tarms with these hyar red-skins?"

"It is my business to be so. I am a trader, and have been among them several months."

"Ye wouldn't mind tryin' to help a feller out of sech a scrape as this that I'm into—would ye?—ef a chance should show itself?"

"I would be glad to assist you, of course; but it would be a difficult thing to do. Have you killed any of the Arapahoes?"

"Nary red-skin. Hain't done 'em a bit of harm—leastways, not on *this* tramp."

"It must have been on some former occasion, then. I heard them say that you were a dangerous enemy."

"It's easy enough to guess what *you* are," thought the hunter. "A minute ago ye 'lowed that I was a red-skin, and now ye say that ye've heerd the 'Rapahoes talkin' about Old Blaze, as well they may. A man who takes to hard lyin' ort to hev a good memory. But I'll give ye a leetle more rope, and see whar ye'll run to."

"Inimy or no inimy," he said, "I know what the critturs are and I know that they're likely to give me the wust kind of a killin' they kin scare up, unless I should happen to slip away from them, and I don't see any chance fur doin' that, without help. Bein' as ye're a white man, I 'lowed ye'd be glad to help a feller creetur in distress."

"Certainly. Any thing I can do will be cheerfully done. But it's a difficult thing, as I told you. The Indians are very angry, and I, if I should be discovered, would share your fate. Besides, the Arapahoes are owing me a large sum. If I should lose it, it would ruin me. I must be very careful, you see, and it is doubtful whether I can accomplish any thing."

"I see that ye're a sneak," thought Old Blaze. "Any white man who was raally white would hev come to see me afore this, and would hev been keen to help me without any axin'. It's jist the easiest thing on airth fur a man to find excuses fur not doin' what he don't want to do."

"Yaas," he said. "I wouldn't hev ye resk yer precious life, stranger, fur twenty doxen skulps like mine; and when it comes to reskin' dollars, why, reckon no mortal man would be so owdacious as to ax *that* of ye. I'm a thousand times obleeged to ye fur yer good wishes, and I make no doubt that ye'll do all ye kin—to keep out of trouble. Will ye be so kind as to tell me—ef thar ain't nothin' dangerous or costly in it—whether thar's an Injun gal livin' hyar, who goes by the name of Dove-eye?"

This question made the trader start. He turned quickly upon the speaker, and his countenance plainly showed the suspicion that had sprung up in his breast.

"Did a snake bite ye, stranger?—or did ye hear suthin'?" inquired Old Blaze.

"What do you want of *her*?" roughly asked Wormley.

"Axin' questions *may* be a good way to help a feller when he's in trouble. Ef it is, stranger, ye're a friend that it'll allers do to bet on. Ef a red-skin should be a-skelpin' of me, I reckon ye'd want to ax how old I was, and what was my mammy's name, afore ye'd pull the crittur off. Then it mought be too late."

"What do you want of Dove-eye? I ask."

"Thar it is ag'in. Old Blaze ain't a bit hard of hearin', or of seein', either. I reckon, from yer way of speakin', that the gal is hyarabouts. What I want of her is, jest to see her and speak to her. Ef ye'll hunt her up and tell her that, it'll be a favor."

"Tell me what business you have with her, and I will send her to you."

"Business! Wal, that beats me! Ain't I in a purty fix, tied up hyar, to 'tend to any kind of *business*? Ef ye allow that I've got a note ag'in the gal, and want her to pay it, ye're as much mistaken as ef ye'd bit yer nose off, thinkin' it mought be a chunk of buffler-hump. But thar's Dove-eye herself, I do believe. Yes; thar ain't no mistakin' *her*, when a man has onct seen her."

The hunter began to telegraph to the girl with great earnestness. Wormley, who saw he was bound to attract the attention of Dove-eye, and who had reasons of his own for not wishing to meet her then and there, turned and walked away.

"That's all the good I'll git out of *him*," muttered Old Blaze. "Wonder ef he ain't a little bit ashamed of hisself. This ole hoss don't mean to forgit him, sartin."

CHAPTER VIII.
A LOVER'S MEETING.

Dove-eye was not as slow of sight as Silas Wormley appeared to be. She noticed the signals of Old Blaze, and came to him as the trader left him.

"Did the white hunter beckon to Dove-eye?" she asked. "I am here. What does he want?"

"Dove-eye is as beautiful as she is brave," replied the hunter, in her own language. "Being beautiful and brave, she must have a heart, and she can feel for those who are in distress. I have been hunted down and captured by the Arapahoes, although I have done them no harm. I did not come here to harm them."

"Dove-eye has seen Burnt Face in battle, and she knows that he is a great brave. He has killed many Arapahoes, and the warriors would be angry if they should lose him. Why was he spying about the village of the Arapahoes?"

"For no harm, I tell you. Has Dove-eye forgotten Silverspur?"

The girl started at this name. The blood mounted to her face in an instant, lighting up the olive of her complexion with a rich glow, and a fierce light came into her large eyes. Then her long eyelashes fell, and a mournful expression overspread her countenance.

"Dove-eye has not forgotten Silverspur," she replied. "Ask the Crows, and let them tell you whether he is forgotten. Their women are still mourning for the warriors who have fallen to avenge the death of Silverspur. Was Burnt Face his friend?"

"I was his friend, and still am. What bird has been whispering lies to Dove-eye? If Silverspur is dead, the Crows know nothing of it."

The light again came into the girl's eyes; the color again mounted to her cheeks, and wild joy and hope showed themselves in every feature.

"The Big Medicine of the Arapahoes told me that he was dead," she replied. "He said that Silverspur was killed by the Crows, and that he saw him slain."

"The Big Medicine lied, or his eyes were blinded. If Silverspur is dead, he was not killed by the Crows. If he is dead, he must have died within two suns, as the sun has not risen twice since I saw him."

"Does Burnt Face speak truly, or does he wish to make the heart of Dove-eye soft, that she may take pity on him?"

"Burnt Face has spoken truly. Does Dove-eye remember, when she fought with her warriors against the Crows on the Sweetwater, when the Crows at last charged upon their enemies, and the Arapahoes were compelled to fly for their lives?"

"Dove-eye has not forgotten. Burnt Face was there."

"Does she remember, when the fighting was over, and she was riding away alone, that she met a white man, and threw her battle-ax at him as she rode past him?"

"I killed him. My battle-ax struck him on the head, and knocked him from his horse."

"You did not kill him. He had been very sick, and he was so weak that he fell from his horse. That white man was Silverspur."

"Yes! Burnt Face speaks truly. I know, now, that it was Silverspur; but he was greatly changed. Is it not two suns since you saw him? He must, then, be not far from here. Where is he?"

Old Blaze described the spot at which he had left his friend, and Dove-eye, her eyes full of joy and eagerness, was about to hasten from him, when he detained her.

"Will not Dove-eye wait a moment?" he asked. "A few minutes will not lose Silverspur. I am a prisoner, and the warriors will kill me, unless I can escape from them."

"Let Burnt Face wait. He has brought me good news, and I will not forget him. If the news is true, he need not fear. I must first see Silverspur."

She sped away, lightly and gracefully as a gazelle, and the hunter gazed after her with admiring eyes.

"I kin trust that gal, sartin," said Old Blaze, relapsing into his vernacular. "Anyhow, she will see Silverspur, and I kin allers bet on *him*. Ef he and that gal put thar wits together, my skulp is safe. I wish that red dog of a white man would come along, so's I could give him a squar' and independent talkin'-to."

But Silas Wormley was engaged in looking after Dove-eye. He had watched her, from the shadow of a lodge, as she conversed with the captive, and he intended to follow her when she stepped away so lightly and gayly.

Dove-eye, eager as she was to greet Silverspur, whom she had so long believed to be dead, had not laid aside the caution which had become a part of her nature. Every now and then she cast stealthy glances behind and about her, to see if her movements were observed, and she soon perceived the espionage of the trader.

It was easy enough to baffle *him*, she thought. Her route lay toward the west, among hills and ravines. She turned toward the south, passed over the brow of a hill in full sight of the trader, and then concealed herself among some bushes in a ravine. In a few moments he came up, and passed her hastily. When she had got him fairly on the wrong track, she emerged from her concealment, and shaped her course toward the west, moving silently and swiftly.

Soon she was in the mountains, before the lodge at the foot of the cliff. She paused a moment; but that was not the place she sought. She went on, up the same ravine that she had climbed with the old medicine-man at the time of the attack by the Crows. She reached the plateau where they had concealed themselves, and there, as she stopped a moment to breathe, from the same clump of cedars in which she had once hid, a man started up before her.

It was Silverspur. She knew him now, although he had changed so much since she saved his life and nursed him while he lay wounded and helpless. She joyfully ran forward to meet him, and he advanced no less eagerly.

"Is this really you, Dove-eye?" he asked, speaking in the Dacotah dialect. "I have been searching for you. I have traveled far to find you. How did you happen to come to this place?"

"I came to meet you. I was told that you were here, and I hastened to see you."

"Who told you?"

"Your friend, Burnt Face."

"You have seen him, then. Where is he?"

"At the village. He is a prisoner."

Silverspur was astonished. Old Blaze a prisoner! He would have anticipated any thing sooner than the capture of the veteran hunter, and this misfortune troubled him greatly.

"The Arapahoes will kill him," he said. "Something must be done. I must save him, if possible, whatever happens."

"He asked me to help him; but I told him that I must first see you. There is time enough to think about him."

"And you hastened to meet me? Had you not forgotten me?"

"Dove-eye had not forgotten. They told me that you were dead—that the Crows had killed you. I vowed to avenge your death upon the Crows, and for that purpose I became a warrior."

"The Crows are my friends. They would never harm me. I was with them at the Sweetwater, when they fought the Arapahoes, and I saw you there."

"Burnt Face told me of that," replied the girl, with a blush. "I threw my battle-ax at you; but I did not know you. I am very sorry."

"It is strange that you were permitted to become a warrior. How did that happen?"

"It is a long story. Do you wish me to tell you all?"

As Silverspur did wish her to tell all, he made her sit by his side, and she related her adventures since they had parted at the lodge in the cliff. She told them briefly and modestly; but there was in them so much that was wonderful and peculiar, so much strength and quickness of mind, so much energy, and so much heroism, that the young man gazed at her in admiration, and could not help interrupting her, now and then, to express his opinion of her achievements.

When she had finished, he sat in silence a few moments, evidently in a "brown study." Then he looked up, and spoke quickly, as a thought occurred to him.

"You are still in danger," he said; "but I think I see a way out of this trouble. You have planned excellently to turn the tables on that trader, and I have no doubt that you will succeed in blinding the eyes of the old men, if he reports what he has discovered; but there is another difficulty. The time is near that you had set for the return of the Big Medicine, and it is not to be supposed that they will submit to any further delay. What did you intend to do, when they should call upon you, a second time, to produce him?"

"I hoped that I would be killed in battle before that time should arrive. Then I thought of flight; but I would have been safe nowhere, and I might as well die here as elsewhere. I expected to die; but the Great Spirit sent you to me, and now I wish to live."

"You might fly with me, and we might escape together, if my friend was free. I can not leave him in danger, and I hardly know what I should do without him. I have a plan by which he can be saved, I believe, and then we will have no more trouble."

"The Great Spirit has surely sent you. What is your plan?"

"What is to prevent us from bringing back the Big Medicine?"

"He is dead."

"We can bring him to life."

"Is the white man's medicine so strong? I would be afraid, if he should return from the spirit-land, that he would tell the warriors how I had deceived them, and then they would be more angry than ever."

"I do not say that I can really bring him back to life. *I* will be the Big Medicine."

The girl uttered an exclamation of joy, as her quick wit caught Silverspur's meaning.

"But he was so old and ugly," she said, "and you are young and—"

"Handsome, you mean, of course. I can stain my face, and can put on gray hair and beard, and I need not let the warriors come near me, and it will be but for a little while. You can tell me what to say—they will be ready to believe almost any thing—and we can be far from here before they will have a chance to discover how they have been cheated."

Dove-eye made many objections to this plan, fearing that it would endanger the life of Silverspur; but he overruled them all, and they went together to the lodge at the foot of the cliff, to arrange the details. She confided in Jose, who promised secrecy and all the assistance that he could render.

It was agreed that Silverspur should take up his abode, for the present, in the cavern in which he had been concealed by Dove-eye when he was wounded. He surveyed the rude apartment with a look of pleasure.

"I have never forgotten this place," he said. "It has always been dear to me, and I am glad to return to it."

"And Dove-eye is happy," replied the girl, blushing as she busied herself in arranging the scanty furniture.

Having given Silverspur her parting directions, and cautioned him not to leave the cavern, she returned to the village.

CHAPTER IX.
DOVE-EYE DENOUNCED.

Silas Wormley was just about to denounce Dove-eye to the old men of the tribe, when he was interrupted by the uproar that preceded the capture of Old Blaze, and which at once emptied the council-house. As it was "bad medicine" to return to the lodge that day, the meeting was postponed until the next morning, when the trader was called before the elders, and requested to proceed with his important communication.

By this time Wormley had "repented him of his wrath." He was sorry that he had been so hasty, and wished that he had given Dove-eye another chance, before going so far as to denounce her. But it was too late to retrieve. The Indians were eager to hear the expected communication, and no excuse would avail.

Rising slowly, and speaking in the inflated style of the savage orators, with which he had become thoroughly familiar, he held forth as follows:

"Let the wise old men listen! The Snake is a friend to the Arapahoes, and they know it. When they were in need, and no other trader would furnish them with powder and lead or cloth and beads, because they were poor, and had no robes with which to pay for what they needed, the heart and the hand of the Snake were open, and he furnished them with every thing they wanted, for themselves and their women. The Snake has always wished well to the Arapahoes, and has never lied to them. Let them now listen to his words.

"There was once a man among the Arapahoes, who was so wise that he was called the Big Medicine. He counseled the people, and they heeded his advice, until he died, and went to the spirit-land."

"The Snake is mistaken," said one of the old men. "The Big Medicine did not die. He went to the spirit-land; but he will return."

"Let the wise men listen! Dove-eye told them, nearly twelve moons ago, that the Big Medicine had gone to the spirit-land, and that he would return in six moons. She had often brought messages to the people from him, and they believed her words. They fought the Crows for a long time, and lost many warriors gaining nothing but a few scalps and horses. When six moons had passed, Dove-eye told the wise men that it would be yet another six moons before he would return. This was hard to believe, and there were some who suspected that Dove-eye was lying to the people. I knew that she was lying, and I am ready to prove it to the wise men."

"The Snake had better be careful how he speaks," said Black Horse. "If he does not speak the truth in this matter, he will suffer for his lies."

"The Snake is not afraid. He is ready to prove his words. The Big Medicine will never return from the spirit-land. He died, and was buried by Dove-eye, with the help of her black slave. I have seen the grave. I have seen the body of the old man. It has lain so long in the ground, that you would not recognize the face; but you would know his white hair and beard and the robe that he wore."

"Let the Snake prove that he has spoken truly."

Wormley mentioned the name of Bull-tail as a witness to what he had seen, and the vagabond was called in. He corroborated Wormley in all particulars, and went further than that worthy, for he described the whipping and choking process by which Jose had been induced to lead them to the grave.

The confidence of the old men in Dove-eye, already weakened, was greatly shaken by this revelation. The trader was not regarded as a man of the strictest veracity, and his witness was entitled to little credit; but they could not believe that he would make such statements, unless he was sure that he had good foundation for them. They determined to bring Dove-eye before the council, and to confront her with her accuser.

The girl listened to the charge, as detailed by the head chief, with the greatest possible composure. When he had ended, she pointed at Wormley, with a glance of ineffable scorn.

"Let the chief believe the words of that man," she said, "and Dove-eye is sure that he will never again be believed among the Arapahoes. Let him believe the words of a lying trader, and the words of a sneaking vagabond who was never believed before. Are these not better than Dove-eye, whom the chief has never known to lie? Let me carry the sand and the wood and elk-chips into the medicine-lodge, and let the warriors cut me in pieces as I pass among them. Come! If Dove-eye has spoken falsely, she is ready to die."

Wormley shrunk back, and the countenance of the chief showed that he was moved by the undaunted demeanor of the girl.

"Why should Dove-eye deceive the people?" he asked. "What could she gain by lying to us?"

"Dove-eye is beautiful," replied the trader. "Many of the young men of the Arapahoes have sought her in marriage; but she would not listen to them, as she thought herself too good to enter the lodge of a warrior. While the

Big Medicine lived, she was allowed to do as she pleased. When he was dead, she wished to become a warrior, that she might still be independent."

"The lying trader does not tell all," said Dove-eye, with another of her scornful glances. "He should also say that he sought me in marriage. When I refused to listen to him, he invented this accusation to destroy me. But this is only talk. Words cost nothing, and it is easy to lie. If the Big Medicine is dead, let the Snake show his grave to the old men. When Dove-eye sees his body, she will be ready to die."

Wormley looked at the girl in astonishment—she was so cool and self-possessed, in view of the fate that awaited her upon the discovery of her imposture. A suspicion entered his mind, for the first time, that his game might not be as certain as he had believed it to be. He knew her to be of a daring spirit and fertile in resources, and he began to fear that she had played him some trick that would confound his plans and render him, instead of her, the victim of the outraged dignity of the Arapahoes.

"Let the trader prove his words," said Black Horse. "Let him lead us to the grave. If the Big Medicine is dead, we will know his body."

There was nothing else for it. Sullenly and reluctantly Wormley led the way out of the council lodge, followed by the old men, and accompanied by Dove-eye and his vagabond accomplice.

He halted in the ravine where he found the grave, and pointed out the spot to the old men. The ground was precisely as he had left it. Even the sharpened stick which he had used for digging lay where he had thrown it. He glanced at Dove-eye, and the half-scornful, half-amused expression of her countenance struck him as strangely out of place.

"Let the wise men dig there," he said, "and they will find the body of the Big Medicine."

Bull-tail was made to throw out the earth from the grave, and he soon uncovered the face and breast of a dead Indian. As he did so, he started back with a look of amazement. Wormley rushed forward, and saw at once that he had been discomfited.

"The Snake has lied to us," said Black Horse. "There is a body here; but it is not that of the Big Medicine. The hair of this man is black, and he has no beard."

Wormley again glanced at Dove-eye, who was smilingly triumphant.

"There has been foul-play here," he said. "The body of the old man has been removed, and this has been put in its place. If the wise men will look, they may find the trail of those who took it away; for it has not been long since it was removed."

Black Horse was incredulous; but he directed a search to be made. No trail could be found, as Jose had not left the slightest trace by which he could be followed.

"I have not lied to the wise men," said Wormley. "Can they suppose that I would have spoken so positively, and that I would have brought them here to see the body of the Big Medicine, unless I had believed it to be here? It *was* here; but it has been cunningly taken away. I saw it lying in that grave, I can swear that I saw the long white hair and the white beard and the curious robe. Bull-tail, too, can swear that he saw them."

The vagabond was about to speak, when Dove-eye turned upon him, with flashing eyes.

"Let the Snake tell his own lies!" she exclaimed. "Do you think the old men will listen to *you*, whose word no man ever believed? Begone, dog of a Pawnee! The old women at the village are waiting to whip you for failing to scrape their kettles."

Bull-tail sneaked away, and Wormley would have followed him; but he was prevented by the chief.

"I have told the old men," continued Dove-eye, "that this trader sought me in marriage, and that he invented this tale to destroy me, because I refused to listen to him. Dove-eye spoke truly when she said that the Big Medicine would return within six moons. He has already returned. I have seen him. If the old men and the warriors will come to the lodge at the foot of the cliff to-morrow morning, they, also, can see him, and can hear him speak."

It lacked but this to fill the measure of Silas Wormley's astonishment and discomfiture. He looked at Dove-eye, and her confident and triumphant air convinced him that she was in earnest, and that she knew the game she was playing.

Black Horse and the other old men received her announcement with the greatest delight. They at once returned to the village, where they caused Wormley to be placed in close confinement.

As soon as possible Dove-eye sought and obtained an interview with Old Blaze, whose case had been overlooked during the investigation of the trader's charges. He had not been forgotten; but a strong guard had been set over him, until the council should decide his fate. Dove-eye briefly told him of her interview with Silverspur, and assured him that he need feel no uneasiness concerning his own safety. She then hastened to the lodge at the foot of the cliff, to rehearse with Silverspur the performance of the next morning.

CHAPTER X.
THE FALSE PROPHET.

It was a joyful procession that left the Arapaho village to visit the old medicine-man. It was a twelvemonth since he had shown his face to the tribe, and their anxiety to see him was most intense. The mysterious and the supernatural profoundly affect the nature of the savage, as well as of the civilized man. The Arapahoes, convinced that their prophet possessed supernatural powers of a high order, were sure that he had come laden with news from the spirit-land, all of which they were eager to hear and prepared implicitly to believe.

Dove-eye, accompanied by Black Horse, led the procession. Next came the old chiefs, the counselors of the tribe, looking as wise and solemn as the occasion demanded, and after them a large concourse of warriors, the women and children not being allowed to take part in the sacred mission.

When they reached the lodge at the foot of the cliff, Dove-eye requested the chief to remain there a few minutes, until she could go in and ascertain whether the Big Medicine was strong enough to receive them; in other words, until she could make sure that Silverspur was prepared to play his part in the performance.

All was ready, and she led the procession into the hut that formed the entrance to the cavern. The rear apartment was not lighted, and the Indians could see nothing until their eyes became accustomed to the darkness. Then they perceived a man, seated on a bench in the cavern, with his face toward them. This man had the death-like complexion of the old medicine-man, as well as his long gray hair and flowing white beard, and was wrapped in the deerskin robe, covered with strange devices, which their prophet had always worn. If there was any thing lacking in the resemblance, their excited imaginations easily supplied the lack.

They recognized him immediately, and were about to step forward and greet him, when he motioned them back by a wave of his hand, and Dove-eye interposed herself at the entrance of the cavern.

"I am very weak, my children," he said, in feeble and broken tones that could not fail to convince his auditors that he spoke truly. "I have long been absent from my people, and during all that time I have not tasted earthly food. In the happy hunting-grounds I was young and strong; but since I have returned, I am older and more feeble than ever. I must eat a great deal of earthly food before I will be strong enough to stand without assistance. I will send Jose to the village, therefore, and you must give him a great load of dried meat and pemmican and meal of the maize, that I may eat and be refreshed."

"It shall be done," replied Black Horse. "Is the Big Medicine satisfied with his children?"

"I would be very well satisfied, if your conduct lately had not given me great pain. You almost refused to believe the message that I sent to you by my child, and you believed the words of a lying trader, when he accused her of having deceived you in my name. Had Dove-eye ever lied to you?"

"Dove-eye had never lied to us. We are sorry that we listened to the talk of the trader, and he shall be burned."

"Let him not be killed. He is a fool, and he has hurt himself more than he has injured Dove-eye. Those who are under the protection of the Great Spirit can not be harmed by any man. The people are owing the Snake for powder and lead and blankets and other articles. Let them release him; but let them give him to understand that they will not pay him any thing, that he has canceled the debt by his lying reports."

A general grunt of assent followed this sage advice, which so easily reconciled the Arapahoes desire of repudiation with their loose ideas of honor.

"Our father gives good advice," said the chief, "and it will surely be heeded. But he seems to have nearly forgotten the language of his people. It is hard to understand all that he says."

"All Indians are at peace in the spirit-land," replied the pseudo prophet, "and all languages are mingled into one, I have been so long speaking the language of the spirit-land, that it is natural to me to use it; but I will soon become accustomed to the speech of my own people."

Silverspur, having been duly tutored by Dove-eve, then mentioned the names of several distinguished warriors who had fallen in battle, and told of their pursuits and progress in the spirit-land, together with the messages which they had sent to their friends—all of which was highly satisfactory to his credulous auditors. He concluded as follows:

"My children have done well to make war upon the Crows, to punish them for their cruel and unprovoked attack, in which so many of our warriors were slain. They have done enough. They have taken a great revenge. The Great Spirit is satisfied, and our warriors in the spirit-land are satisfied. Let them now make peace with the Crows."

"What our father tells us is hard to do," replied Black Horse. "If we should now send to the Crows to ask for peace, they would kill the messengers."

"You have a white captive, whom you call Burnt Face. He is a friend of the Crows, and has great influence among them. Release him, and send him to the Crows, and he will make peace for you."

"The Big Medicine knows every thing. It shall be as he says. Does our father wish to say any thing more to his children?"

"Nothing; except that you must not visit me again until six suns have passed. Then I will be strong and well, and I can take my children by the hand and talk to them."

The Indians silently left the lodge, and the procession wended its way down the mountain. Dove-eye watched them until they were out of sight, and then hastened back to Silverspur, who had thrown aside his disguise.

"Was it well done?" he asked, as he greeted her joyfully "Do you think they can suspect any thing wrong?"

"It was very well done. Silverspur is a wonderful man. Why did you tell them that they must not come here again until after six suns?"

"By that time, I hope, we will be far from here. I wished to keep them from molesting us when we leave."

"I had guessed that. Why did you ask the chief for a big load of dried meat and pemmican and maize meal?"

"So that we can have plenty to eat on our journey, and need not stop to hunt."

"I can understand that, too. But why did you tell them to let the Snake go?"

"He has not really done any harm, although he wished to do harm. If he loses his money, that will be a sufficient punishment for him. You must go to the village, Dove-eye, and see if all is going on well there, and if they released Burnt Face. If they do release him, send him or bring him here; but he ought not to be seen coming here."

Old Blaze had been released from captivity before Dove-eye reached the village, and was in the council-lodge with the old men, who were giving him instructions concerning his mission to the Crows. He had been greatly astonished at the turn his affairs had taken, but had prudently kept his astonishment to himself. He was sure that Silverspur and Dove-eye had had something to do with his release, and he resolved not to do or say any thing that might interfere with their plans.

When the chief told him that he had been informed that the Burnt Face was a friend of the Crows, and that he would be willing to undertake a mission of peace to them from the Arapahoes, he guessed who the informant was, and readily assented to both propositions. He only asked that his rifle should be returned to him, and expressed his willingness to set forth at any moment. Having received his instructions as ambassador, he was dismissed from the council-lodge, and soon met Dove-eye in the village. She said only a word to him, and left him, but joined him after a little while, in a ravine a short distance from the village. She then led him to the lodge at the foot of the cliff, giving him, by the way, a brief outline of the doings of Silverspur and herself.

The hunter thanked his friend for his rescue, and complimented him upon his tact and adroitness.

"It was nothing," replied Silverspur "It was only fun to me, and I was really quite selfish about it. It was necessary to get Dove-eye out of the scrape, and you know that I could not get along without you."

"It's a heap to me, boy, and I'm obleeged to ye all the same. Here I am, a-livin', and I've got old Jule back, too, when I didn't hev the least idee that I'd ever set eyes onto the old critter ag'in."

He caressed his rifle affectionately, and accepted an invitation to smoke.

"Ye've done wrong," he continued, "'cordin' to my notion, in lettin' that tradin' crittur go. Ef the red-skins wanted to kill him, I don't believe this child would hev hindered 'em."

"Would you wish them to murder a fellow-creature—a man of our own race?"

"I don't call it murder to kill snakes. I don't consider that chap a feller-crittur, and he ain't a man of my race, sartin. He lacks a heap of bein' a white man, and he's wuss'n a red-skin. Even a Digger Injun would try to help another Digger out of trouble; but that tradin' chap wouldn't lift a finger to save yer skulp, unless he was well paid fur it. I know what he's made of, and it's the kind o' timber, to my notion, that ort to burn. Ef he had had his way, Dove-eye would hev been chopped into little pieces by this time."

"But she is safe, and he can do no more harm. We will soon be far from here."

"I'd like to give the crittur a talkin' to afore I go. When do ye allow to leave?"

"To-morrow. We can hardly get ready to start to-night. Jose must go to the village and bring us a load of provisions. Your horse and mine are safe where we left them. You must make the Indians give you at least two horses to carry you to the Crows. Jose will get one for himself, and that will be enough to carry ourselves and our plunder."

"Are ye goin' to take that thar niggur?"

"Yes. He wishes to follow his mistress, and she wishes it, too. We will start in the morning, if you see no objection to that move. We will have a clear field for a start, and it will be several days, I think, before the Arapahoes find out that we are gone."

"I don't see nothin' to hinder. It's all right, as fur as I kin calkilate; but I wish ye'd let the Injuns take keer of that trader. I don't like his looks, and he reminds me, somehow, of a chap I once met, many year ago, who did me a heap of harm."

"What was that, old friend?"

"I don't like to talk about it; but I married and settled down once, when beaver was high, and I had made a good pile by trappin'. My wife was a Delewar' woman, and what ye mought call handsome. People didn't call me Old Blaze then; but I was known as Ben Farrar—*Mister* Ben Farrar. Thar come along a tradin' chap named Bob Riley, and he run off with my squaw afore I'd well got to know who he was. I mought hev got along well enough without the woman; but she kerried off my boy with her, and he was a powerful pert little chap. It went hard with me to lose him, and I follered up thar trail right sharp; but they went into the settlements, and I had to give it up. That busted up my settlin', and I've been a tol'abul wild crittur ever sence."

"Do you say that the trader reminds you of that man?"

"Kinder. The more I think of it, the more I see the favor. Ef he don't keep out of my way, his looks may kill him yit. Wal, I must be gittin' down to the village."

CHAPTER XI.
NOT UNWHIPT OF JUSTICE.

Silas Wormley was as much astonished at his release as Old Blaze had been at receiving a similar favor. He had fully expected that the Indians would mete out to him the same fate that would have awaited Dove-eye if he had succeeded in exposing her imposture, and he saw no way to extricate himself from the dilemma.

When he was informed that he was released by the order of the Big Medicine, he had his guess at the truth of the matter, as the hunter had had his. He perceived that Dove-eye had outwitted him, and he felt a strong desire to "get even" with her. This desire was intensified when he was further informed that the Arapahoes, in accordance with the direction of the Big Medicine, had determined not to pay what they were owing him, considering his false accusations, a receipt in full for all indebtedness. This was touching him in the pocket; it was ruining him in business, and he resolved that the matter should not rest as Dove-eye had left it.

Making inquiries in the village, he learned all the particulars of the visit to the lodge of the Big Medicine. He wondered at the shrewdness of Dove-eye, no less than at the credulity of the Indians. He had received a practical, matter-of-fact education, and had been brought up with a contempt for witchcraft, ghost-seers, prophecies, and all that savored of the supernatural. It would have been as impossible to make him believe that the Big Medicine had been to the spirit-land and returned, as to convince him that the Arapahoes had cut his head off. He knew that Dove-eye had been deceiving the people, and he felt that both principal and interest (of the debts the Arapahoes owed him) required him to expose the imposture. He knew, also, that it would never do for him to make a second failure, as death would surely be the penalty for another unsuccessful attempt. Nevertheless, he was willing to run some risk. Although he would not wet his feet to save the life of a fellow-man, he would dive to recover his pocket-book.

Had the old medicine-man been alive and concealed all this time, and had the girl been acting only as his instrument in the deception, or had she some other confederate, who had personated the Big Medicine? It could not be that the old man was alive, for he had seen him lying in his grave. The trader had no doubt of this, although the body had been so cunningly spirited away, he had never seen the old man in life; but Bull-tail could not have wished to deceive him. The hair, the features and the dress of the body corresponded exactly with the descriptions of the Big Medicine, and he had noticed a medal lying on his breast, which he had frequently heard mentioned and described. Besides, if the body had not been that of the Big Medicine, Dove-eye would not have taken the trouble to remove it and put another in its place. She had another confederate, and who was he?

Silas Wormley was shrewd enough; but his heart and brain were so contracted, that his shrewdness was exercised only on a small scale, he suspected that Dove-eye's confederate was a white man, and there were two circumstances that confirmed him in that suspicion. The Big Medicine, he was told, had spoken quite imperfectly the dialect used by the Arapahoes, and the lame excuse which he had given, although it had easily satisfied the credulous Indians, had another effect upon Silas Wormley. Again—why had he directed the Arapahoes to release Old Blaze, about whom he seemed to know so much? What was the hunter doing when he was captured near the village? For what purpose had he come there? The trader knew that white men on the plains, like snakes, are generally found in couples. When one is seen, there is another not far from him.

Putting this and that together, his natural shrewdness stimulated by his desire for money and for Dove-eye, the trader concluded that there must be a white man at the bottom of the mystery, and that the white man was concealed at the lodge of the Big Medicine, he determined to reconnoiter that position, and to make such discoveries as he could, with as little danger to himself as possible.

He set out, accordingly, at a late hour in the evening, and went direct to the lodge at the foot of the cliff. Finding no entrance except through the hut, he crept as near to it as he dared, for the purpose of peeping and listening.

His enterprise was rewarded. He heard two voices, one of which he recognized as Dove-eye's, and the other was that of a man. Yes, it was a white man's voice; there was no mistaking the tone and the accent. He could not hear what they were saying; but they laughed merrily every now and then, and he had no doubt that they were discussing the events of the morning.

He was about to creep up closer; but he heard Dove-eye, as she moved toward the entrance, say that she must return to the village, and he was obliged to hasten away and conceal himself.

He watched the girl until she was out of sight, and then decided that he would make a closer examination of the lodge, in order to satisfy himself who and what the white man was.

There was an obstacle in his way. As he emerged from his hiding place, he was confronted by a dark and stalwart form.

It was the negro, Jose. In one hand he held a stout stick, and in the other he carried a leather thong.

"I saw you coming," he said, "and I watched you. You whipped Jose, and now it is Jose's turn to whip you."

The trader hastily drew a pistol from his belt; but Jose's stick knocked it from his hand before he could cock it. The next instant he was struggling in vain to release himself from the brawny arms of the negro.

"You had better be quiet," said Jose. "If you make any noise, I will kill you. Go on!"

Having securely tied the hands of his victim, Jose flourished his stick over his head, and led him, holding the end of the leather thong, down into a thickly wooded ravine, where he fastened him to a tree. He then cut some tough switches, and addressed himself to his work.

Wormley begged piteously that his back might be spared, and then tried bribes and threats; but all without effect upon the obdurate negro, whose reply was always the same.

"You whipped Jose, and Jose means to whip you."

And he did whip him. He plied his switches so effectually, that the trader squirmed and writhed, and cried and screamed, and called vainly for help. It was not until the negro had exhausted his switches, and had gone to procure a fresh supply that the victim had any respite. He anxiously looked around, hoping that somebody might have heard his appeals for help, and was delighted to see a man coming down the ravine toward him.

As it was dusk, he could not distinguish the features of the stranger until he came nearer, when he perceived that it was the white captive who had asked his aid in the village. At the same moment the negro returned with more switches.

Seeing the white man, Jose hesitated for a moment; but, as Old Blaze calmly seated himself on a log, and showed no disposition to interfere, he proceeded to administer another dose of the oil of hickory.

"Won't you take this nigger off of me, mister?" entreated Wormley. "He has been torturing me more than half an hour and you see that he means to begin again."

"Are ye right shore that it's more'n half an hour?" replied the hunter. "Do ye kerry a watch, stranger?"

"The exact time is a matter of no consequence. You see what he has done. Don't you mean to stop him?"

"I'm mighty sorry to see ye in that fix, stranger, and would like to help ye; but it's a difficult thing to do."

"It is very easy, if you wish to do it."

"Thar ain't no tellin' how much I want to help you. War ye a-doin of any harm to the niggur?"

"None at all."

"I've heern tell that that niggur has got a grudge ag'in ye, 'cause ye gin him a powerful whalin' and chokin' a while ago. That niggur is mad, and it mought be dangerous fur me to interfere with him."

Jose stopped the colloquy by applying a few more stripes, and then the trader again besought the aid of Old Blaze.

"I tell ye that I'm mons'ous sorry to see ye in this fix," replied the hunter. "What more kin ye ax? I shouldn't wonder ef that niggur is five or six pound heavier than I am, and ye wouldn't want me to resk my life by buttin' ag'in him."

"If you have the heart of a man, you will not allow him to torment me any longer."

"I've got abundance of heart, stranger. In fact, my heart is bigger than a skinned hoss; but I'm kinder afeard. That thar niggur mought be owin' me suthin sometime, and p'raps, ef I should interfere with him now, he wouldn't be willin' to pay me."

"Jose has whipped you for himself," said the negro. "He must now whip you for Dove-eye."

He proved his zeal in the cause of his mistress by administering a dozen more blows, well laid on, and then he turned his victim loose.

"I'm glad that ye're well orter that scrape, stranger," said Old Blaze, rising to his feet. "Now I want ye to answer me one question. 'Pears like I've seen ye somewhar, sometime. Did ye ever go by the name of Bob Riley?"

The trader turned a frightened, suspicious glance upon his questioner, and then with a cry of alarm, ran at full speed down the ravine. Old Blaze quickly raised his rifle to his shoulder, but lowered it after a moment's thought.

"It would bring the Injuns down on us," he muttered, "and that mought upset some of Silverspur's plans. But I do believe it is the same chap."

He walked up to Dove-eye's lodge, followed by Jose, who was supremely gratified at having been allowed to work out his revenge without hindrance.

Silas Wormley, however, was by no means gratified or satisfied. When he believed himself beyond the pursuit of Old Blaze, he slackened his speed, but did not stop until he was safe in the village and in his own lodge. His back smarted to such an extent that he could not sleep, and he passed a restless night, thinking of his degrading and painful punishment, and revolving plans of vengeance.

He was determined to be revenged, cost what it might, upon the negro, as well as upon Dove-eye and the white man whom he believed to be her confederate. There was but one way of accomplishing this—to expose completely the deception that had been practiced. He was afraid to prosecute his search while Old Blaze was in the neighborhood; but the hunter was to go away at an early hour in the morning, and then the coast would be clear.

He did not stir from his lodge until Old Blaze had left the village, and then he waited until evening before he ventured up into the mountains. He went armed, to defend himself against Jose, intending that the negro should not again take him at a disadvantage.

He carefully reconnoitered the lodge of Dove-eye before he ventured to approach it, but saw nothing to indicate that it was inhabited. He went nearer, and the same quiet and absence of incident prevailed. At length he went to the hut, and looked in at the door, when he saw that the tenement was deserted. He entered it, and the sight that met his eyes convinced him that his suspicions had been well founded.

Among other evidences of a hasty departure, he saw a quantity of long white hair on the stone floor of the cavern in the rear, and a robe of deerskin, covered with strange devices. A closer search revealed a spur lying in one corner—a large and handsome spur, of solid silver, with a steel rowel. This had been, without doubt, the property of Dove-eye's white confederate.

Leaving things as he had found them, Wormley hastened back to the village, and told the head chief what he had discovered. Black Horse listened to him with the greatest incredulity, and it was not until he had repeated his story, with the strongest possible asseverations of its truth, that the chief could be induced to call together the old men.

The trader argued his cause before them with great earnestness, feeling that his money and his revenge, if not his life, were now depending on his success, and at last they reluctantly consented to pay a visit to the lodge of the Big Medicine.

When they reached the lodge, however, and saw the proofs that Wormley had to show them, they were not as easily convinced as he had expected them to be. The cherished belief of many years was not to be demolished at one blow. Even the spur of silver, which he triumphantly exhibited to them, did not shake their confidence in Dove-eye.

"I know the white man who wore this," said Black Horse as he held up the spur. "He is named Silverspur. He is a great warrior, and is a friend of the Crows. He may have been here. He may have captured Dove-eye and carried her away. If he has been here, that does not prove that the Big Medicine is dead, or that Dove-eye has deceived the people."

"If the Big Medicine is alive," replied the trader, "where is he? He was so weak that he could not move, and no one was to be allowed to touch him for six suns; but he is not here."

"He may have gone out to walk," suggested the chief, "or the white men may have captured both him and Dove-eye. Dove-eye is very beautiful, and the Big Medicine is very wise. The white people would be very glad to have both of them."

Wormley was disgusted at this view of the subject, which seemed to him to be the hight of unreason. He began to despair of carrying his point, and it is probable that the investigation would have been abandoned, but for an unforeseen occurrence.

Two warriors, who had been sent to search for trails in the vicinity, returned and reported that they had came upon a grave that had been recently made. Surprised to find a grave in that locality, they had examined it, and had discovered the body of the Big Medicine.

At this announcement the old men hurried off in undignified haste to visit the grave, and found that the report of the warriors was true. Their demeanor changed instantly. They loaded Wormley with praises and promises, and could not find language severe enough for their denunciation of Dove-eye and her confederates.

The warriors were sent out to hunt for the trail of the fugitives, and they soon discovered, at a little distance from the lodge, a place where horses had been kept, and from which the start had evidently been made. They followed the trail a little way, and reported that six horses had gone toward the north.

Black Horse returned to the village in hot haste, to organize a war party for the pursuit of the runaways; but it was night when he was ready, and the trail could not be taken up until morning.

CHAPTER XII.
"THE GOVERNOR."

As Wormley suspected, the departure of Silverspur and his companions had been sudden and hasty. Old Blaze, on his arrival, related the adventure of the trader with Jose, and the negro said that he had caught the trader spying about the vicinity of the lodge.

As it was evident that he could be there for no good purpose, that he was bent on discovering Dove-eye's secret and making it known to the Indians, the party concluded that they had better set out that night, instead of waiting until morning.

Few preparations were needed, and they set out at midnight, mounted on four good horses, with two led animals, that were taken in charge by Old Blaze and Jose. The night was very dark; but Dove-eye knew every foot of the country in that vicinity, and led them down the mountain by the nearest practicable route. When they were fairly out of the hills, Old Blaze took the lead, and the party rode at a good rate of speed toward the north.

They rode steadily during the night and all through the next day, stopping only at sunrise and at noon for rest and refreshment, more for the benefit of their horses than themselves. When night came, they were in sight of the Black Hills, having traveled more than eighty miles, according to the calculation of Old Blaze, and Silverspur proposed that they should encamp for the night upon an elevation near the creek whose course they had been following.

"Better not," said the hunter. "The 'Rapahoes are on our trail, no doubt, long afore this, and they will make better time than we do, 'cause they will all hev led hosses, and kin change from tired to fresh when they want to."

"We have such a start, it seems to me that they will hardly try to follow us, even if they miss us."

"Don't ye bet too high on that, boy. Ye're fooled ef ye think they wouldn't miss ye, and that right soon. I tell ye, that tradin' chap is mad, and he's bound to make mischief. He's a coward, no doubt; but I reckon the mad in him is bigger'n the coward, by this time. Ye did a wrong thing when ye told the Injuns to turn him loose, and I did a wrong thing when I didn't shoot him down arter drawin' a bead onto him."

"We may have made a mistake. If we did, it was on the side of mercy, and that is the best side."

"Yaas. I don't know nothin' about marcy when I butt up agin' Injuns and snakes; but it's a pity that that snake wasn't killed. The red-skins will be madder than any hornets when they find out the truth of the matter, and the start we've got won't amount to much. I reckon we'd better keep on travelin'."

"But Dove-eye must be tired. Such a long ride without rest is enough to exhaust any one."

"It ain't too much fur a warrior. I'm keen to bet that the gal has traveled a longer stretch than this, when she was fightin' the Crows."

"Dove-eye is not tired," replied the maiden, with a blush at the allusion.

"I'm tired myself, then," rejoined Silverspur, "and I mean to camp."

"Just as ye please. Any thin' 'll suit this ole hoss. I was only speakin' for yer own good."

They encamped, accordingly, on the elevation that Silverspur had pointed out, and the night was passed in rest and tranquility. Early in the morning they resumed their journey; but it was not long before they came to a halt, on descrying a large body of horsemen approaching them from the north.

"Who are those, old friend?" asked Silverspur. "They can hardly be your Arapahoes, as they would not be likely to come upon us from that direction."

"Not 'Rapahoes, but Injuns fur all that," replied the hunter.

"They are too many for us, then. Hadn't we better turn toward the hills and get out of their way?"

"They are friends."

"How do you know that?"

"Your young eyes ort to be better than my old 'uns. Cain't ye see that thar's white men among 'em?"

"I believe I do, since you have mentioned it."

"Sogers, too, and those Injuns are Crows."

The hunter was right, as was revealed by the closer approach of the party. It was composed of some fifty warriors, finely mounted, and arrayed in all their barbaric splendor, accompanied by twenty dragoons of the United States service and two or three officers. They had halted when they descried Silverspur and his friends, but had continued their course on perceiving that there were white men in the party.

"The devil is to pay now!" exclaimed Silverspur, as he reined in his horse, and came to a sudden stop.

"What's the matter?" asked Old Blaze, noticing his young friend's look of vexation.

"There's the governor."

"Governor who? What governor?"

"My father—Colonel Wilder—that officer on the gray horse."

"Thunderation! Is Colonel Wilder your father? I should think you'd be glad to see the old gen'leman."

"But I'm not—just now."

"Why's that? We needn't be afeard of the 'Rapahoes now. Thar's Crows and sogers enough to take keer of us."

"I had rather meet the Arapahoes. We might get away from them. The governor may be too inquisitive," concluded Silverspur, with a significant glance at Dove-eye.

"Thar's suthin' in that, shore enough. Colonel Wilder don't look like a man who would fancy an Indian wife for his son. Do ye raaly mean to marry the gal?"

"I hope to. It is certain that I will never marry any other."

"That is talkin' like a man. Wal, my boy, what will be will be, and thar's no use in frettin'. Hyar they are, and we've got to meet 'em."

Colonel Wilder came riding forward in advance of his party accompanied by Bad Eye, the head chief of the Crows. The colonel was an old gentleman of fine appearance, who looked as if he had been born to fill the position of an officer. In fact, he had been a hard fighting and hard working soldier, who had fought and worked his way up to the grade which he then held and well deserved. He was dressed in his full uniform—an unusual thing with an officer on duty in the wilderness, and his appearance produced a feeling of respectful awe even in Old Blaze, who was not accustomed to such feelings.

He did not recognize his son until he was quite close to him, and it was evident—although he controlled himself, and returned Fred's greeting very cordially—that he was surprised to see him at that place and in such company.

"Why, Fred!" he exclaimed, "you are the last man I would have expected to meet here. I thought that you had quit this wild life, and that you had settled down to business in St. Louis."

"I thought so, too, sir, for a while, and I believe I tried to settle down; but every thing was so strange to me in the city, and I felt an unconquerable desire to return to the free life of the plains."

"An unconquerable desire! I must confess my ignorance of the meaning of that phrase. I am afraid that you have grown to be a perfect savage. Who are your friends, and where are you going?"

"This is Old Blaze, father. Don't you know him?" replied Fred, turning to the hunter.

"Yes. I have seen him once, and have often heard of him. But who are the others? Is that his squaw?"

"I believe not," evasively replied Fred. "But where are you going, sir?" he asked, anxious to change the subject of conversation. "I should judge from your uniform, that you were on your way to pay a visit of ceremony."

"You have guessed it. The Crows and the Arapahoes have been fighting for a long time, and have made it dangerous for travelers to cross the plains. It is my duty to try to patch up a peace between them. I have brought some of the principal men of the Crows, and we mean to pay a visit to the Arapahoes and have a big talk. You know the effect, in such proceedings, of an officer's full dress uniform."

Silverspur and Old Blaze looked at each other. If they could not get away from Colonel Wilder and his party, they must meet the enraged Arapahoes, who, as they could not doubt, were hot on their trail. It was an awkward dilemma for Fred Wilder, and it soon became still more awkward.

One of the Crow chiefs took Colonel Wilder aside, and conversed with him in a low tone. Dove-eye was the subject of their conversation, as they both glanced at her frequently, and the officer looked surprised and interested.

"Is there no mistake about this?" he asked, turning to Bad Eye. "I am told that that girl is an Arapaho, and that she has been fighting the Crows as a warrior."

"It is true. She has been a warrior," replied the chief, who was gazing intently at Dove-eye.

"It is very strange. What is she doing, my son, in *your* company?"

"The truth is," desperately replied Fred, "that I am trying to save her from the Arapahoes. They would kill her, if they should get her in their power."

"This is still more strange. She has unsexed herself by fighting in their ranks, and now they wish to kill her. What has she done?"

"It is a long story, sir—so long that I have no time to tell it now. Let us pass on. Our doing so will save her life, and will not interfere with your mission."

"I shall not allow it. There is more in this, Fred, than you are willing to tell me, and I mean to get at the truth. She is a fine-looking girl, the handsomest squaw I ever saw. In fact, she does not look like an Indian. Have you taken her from her people against her will?"

"No sir."

"You have taken her, then, against *their* will."

"I suppose I must admit that."

"The truth is coming out, I see. Fred Wilder, reckless scapegrace as you are, I always believed you to be a gentleman, a man of honor. I never supposed that you could stoop so low as to take a mean advantage of any woman, even of a poor Indian girl."

"Have you seen any thing to cause you to change your opinion?" proudly replied the young man.

"I ask you again, what is this Indian girl doing in your company? You have taken her from her people, and you are afraid that they will pursue you and take her back. What do you want to do with her?"

"I mean to make her my wife."

Astonishment is no word for the emotion that showed itself in Colonel Wilder's countenance, in his whole frame. He was stupefied; he was thunderstruck. He fairly staggered under the blow and turned pale and red by turns.

"Have you taken leave of your senses?" he exclaimed. "Do you mean what you say—or have you become so entirely an Indian, that you have no regard for the truth?"

"I never lie, sir," coolly replied Fred. The murder was out, now, and he had nerved himself to hear the worst.

"Do you suppose that I will consent to such a thing? Can you suppose, for a moment, that I will consent to become the grandfather of a tribe of half-breeds?"

Fred's eyes twinkled; but he said nothing.

"And you, a Wilder!—my son! How can you think of so disgracing yourself?"

"You have often told me, sir, that you wished me to marry and settle down."

"Did I ever wish you to marry a squaw, and to settle in a wigwam? Let me hear nothing more of this nonsense. You will remain with me, until we meet the Arapahoes."

"I can not do it, sir. They will kill Dove-eye."

"Is that her name? Dove-eye! How very romantic! Her husband, from whom you took her, may correct her in the Indian fashion; but I will warrant you there will be no killing done. Will you do as I request you to do?"

"I can not promise, sir."

"I must order you, then. You will please to remember that I, within the limits of my command, am 'monarch of all I survey.' Unless you agree to obey me, I will order my dragoons to arrest you and keep you under restraint."

"The United States service may lose a dragoon or two, before that is done."

"Indeed! We will see, sir."

Fred Wilder looked rebellious, and the dispute might have terminated disastrously to somebody, if it had not been interrupted by some strange conduct on the part of the Crow chief and Dove-eye.

CHAPTER XIII.
KATE ROBINETTE.

It was Bad Eye, the old head chief of the Crows, who first interrupted the belligerent conversation between Silverspur and his father.

It should be remarked here, that the interview took place in the edge of a belt of timber, near a creek, and that nearly all had dismounted, some tethering their horses, and others allowing them to graze at will. Among those who had dismounted were the Indian girl and Bad Eye.

The chief had been gazing a long time at Dove-eye, with an expression of interest that he did not attempt to conceal, and she, without meeting his fixed gaze, had glanced at him, now and then, wonderingly and strangely. He had drawn nearer to her, and his interest increased the longer and the closer he looked at her. At last he spoke, uttering but one word:

"Kate!"

The girl started and turned around quickly. The chief's arms were extended, and, with a wild cry, she rushed into them.

It was this that interrupted the conversation of Fred and his father, and brought a new element into the scene.

"How is this?" exclaimed Colonel Wilder, turning around, with his eyes open wide. "What is the matter with the chief? You seem to have a rival here, Fred, or something else."

The young man, who was as much at a loss as his father was, discreetly said nothing.

The chief, who was holding Dove-eye in a close embrace, released her, but held her hand. The Crow warriors were stolidly silent, because it was their custom to betray no emotion. The dragoons were silent, because they had not been ordered to speak, and they sat quietly on their horses, wondering what it all meant. Fred Wilder was silent, because he believed that he had better not speak, and that any turn of affairs could not be for the worse. Old Blaze was silent, because he implicitly believed in Silverspur's ability to talk himself out of any scrape. Jose was silent, because he understood nothing of what was going on. Bad Eye and the Indian girl were silent, because their emotion had not yet found vent in words.

Colonel Wilder, in fact, was the only noisy man in the party. His anxiety concerning his son, and his curiosity to learn the meaning of this last demonstration, impelled him to ask the chief a multitude of questions, which the latter seemed to be in no hurry to answer.

"Do you remember Paul Robinette?" asked Bad Eye, at last, and speaking in very good English.

"The fur-trader? Yes; I knew him well."

"You may remember that he was killed and scalped, on the plains, by the Blackfeet, who carried off his daughter."

"Yes; but you don't mean to say that this girl is Flora Robinette? She was found, and is married to Captain Benning—though I don't know why they call him captain. He has a trading-post on the other side of the mountains, and she is living there with him."

"Precisely so. After Silverspur rescued Flora Robinette from the Blackfeet—"

"Who is Silverspur?" interrupted the colonel.

"Your son—Fred Wilder."

"Savage in name, as well as in nature. Go on."

"After he rescued her from the Blackfeet, she was again captured by the Arapahoes. In seeking her among them, he was badly hurt, and his life was saved by this girl. But I am making a long story of it. Flora Robinette had a sister."

"That is news to me. You seem to be coming to the point."

"The truth is I have commenced at the wrong end of my story, and must begin again. Did you ever see Paul Robinette's brother?"

"I saw him once, many years ago. He disappeared mysteriously."

"I am he. I had good cause, as I believe, to forsake my brother; but I will not bring up old grudges now. To be revenged upon him, I took with me his child, a daughter, Flora's elder sister. She lived with me among the Crows, several years; but one day she was missing, and I could find no trace of her from that day to this. I have found her to-day. I called her by the old familiar name. She remembered it, and she knew me, as I had recognized her."

"Very romantic! If I was an author, I would write a tale."

"I was going to say, when I commenced my story at the wrong end, that when Flora was finally safe, I informed her of my relationship, in the presence of your son and Captain Benning, and told her that she had had a sister; but I did not then expect that I would ever see Kate."

- 64 -

"Very good. And you are chief of the Crows, and she will be a great lady in the tribe, no doubt. I am very glad you have found her, and hope you will keep her. We may as well camp here and get something to eat. Lieutenant Rawlings, dismount your men, and form a corral. I hope, Fred, that you will now remain with us. If the Arapahoes come, Bad Eye will not be likely to give up his niece to them, and the Crow warriors will take an interest in her, I am sure."

As Colonel Wilder had so summarily dismissed the subject, no one attempted to revive it, and all busied themselves in preparations for encamping. Hardly were these completed, when some Crows, who had been looking for game in the vicinity, announced that they had discovered a large herd of buffalo, on the plain at a little distance from the camp. All were excited by this intelligence, especially Colonel Wilder.

"This is glorious!" he exclaimed. "Now we will have a grand surround!"

The rest of the party, both white and red, were as eager for the hunt as was Colonel Wilder, and a grand surround was determined upon.

Leaving a sufficient number of dragoons to guard the camp, Bad Eye led the rest of the party to the buffalo ground. The prospect of a surround was so exciting, that every other topic was laid aside, and all pressed forward eagerly to join the chase.

Under the direction of the Crow chief, his warriors taking the lead, the herd was gradually surrounded, the hunters keeping carefully out of sight of the game, until the buffalo were inclosed in a great circle, more than a mile in circumference. Then, at a signal passed from one to another around the circle, all began to move toward the center, slowly closing in upon their expected victims. When they were perceived by the buffalo, the excitement of the sport commenced, and increased rapidly from that moment. Seeing their natural enemies on one side, the frightened animals went at a gallop to the other, where they were driven back by the sight of more men. Then they rushed frantically from one part of the plain to another, only to be met on every side by a steady wall of their foes, who had drawn so close together that they presented the appearance of a line of battle.

As a last resort the herd collected in the center of the circle, and seemed to be searching for a weak point, at which they could break through the line that surrounded them. If such was their intention, they were too late in carrying it into execution; for their enemies, at a given signal, dashed down upon them in a mass.

Right into the midst of the herd went the red and white riders, each singling out his victim, and endeavoring to keep at his side until a suitable opportunity should present itself to deliver a death-shot. The maddened buffalo started off at a tearing gallop, and the scene that followed possessed sufficient danger and excitement to charm the wildest and most reckless hunter. Nothing could be seen, for some time, but the immense mass of animals, surging forward and heaving like the waves of the ocean, and nothing could be heard but the bellowings of rage or pain, and the shouts and shots of their slaughterers.

In such a *mêlée* the men inevitably became separated from each other, and each for himself was a law of necessity. If a man sought to keep on the outskirts of the herd, he might find himself within it the next moment, and he might be carried with it until some fortunate chance should give him an opening to escape. If he was a greenhorn, or a poor horseman, or if any accident should befall himself or his horse, he might be thrown down in the midst of the frightened herd, and perhaps trampled to death. The sport was as dangerous as it was exciting; but none held off from it on account of the danger.

Colonel Wilder, who was an ardent sportsman, and who, notwithstanding his years, believed himself to be equal to the best, showed a skill and prowess that were surpassed by none on the ground. Dashing at once into "the thick" of the herd, he selected a fine cow, and, watching his opportunity, delivered a death-shot that dropped her "in her tracks." He then ranged up alongside of a large bull; but his horse swerved as he fired, and the animal was only wounded. The bull turned and charged furiously, the colonel's horse snorted and reared, the saddle-girth burst, and he fell to the ground, while the horse galloped frantically away with the herd.

It was a perilous situation, and Colonel Wilder fully appreciated his danger. The herd had gone by, and there was no fear that he would be trampled to death; but the wounded bull had lowered his head for a charge, to which no effectual resistance could be opposed, and it was useless to attempt to escape.

As the buffalo charged, the colonel struck at him with the butt of his rifle; but the weapon broke over his shaggy frontlet, with no more effect than the breaking of a straw would have had. The bull struck the barrel, however, between his horns, and Colonel Wilder was thus saved from serious injury, although he was knocked down and badly bruised.

As the bull lowered his head for a charge that would finish his prostrate antagonist, Colonel Wilder gave himself up for lost. He closed his eyes, and mentally ejaculated a prayer for help.

Help came, as timely as it was unexpected. There was a shot, and the bull never reached his foe. The bullet had struck him just behind the fore-shoulder, and had penetrated his heart.

The colonel looked up, and his eyes were fastened on the dying struggles of the buffalo. The immense beast, with blood streaming from his mouth and nostrils, with his tongue protruding, and with the glaze of death already over his bloodshot eyes, seemed determined to "stand his ground" to the last. As his huge body swayed from side to side, and he found himself unable to move a pace from where he stood, he planted his feet further apart, and stamped impatiently, as if angry at the growing weakness which it was impossible to shake off. But all his efforts were in vain. Death was too strong to be resisted by his brute force and tenacious will. The purple blood gushed in a torrent from his mouth, the huge carcass swayed more heavily from side to side, the failing limbs shook in a final effort to support the weight of the body, the whole frame was seized with a convulsive quiver, and at last, with a choking gasp, the animal fell over, dead, silent, motionless and stiff.

Colonel Wilder gave a sigh of relief when the struggle was over, and looked around for his preserver. Dove-eye was standing near him, with a rifle in her hand, watching the death of the buffalo with great composure. As she was about to walk away, the colonel rose and addressed her:

"I am much obliged to you, sir. You have saved my life. Ah! is it you, young woman? Excuse me; my eyes are a little dim. Did you really fire that shot?"

Dove-eye smiled and nodded.

"You must be an excellent marksman—woman, I mean. The variation of an inch would have left strength enough in that animal to kill me."

"Are you hurt?"

"Not at all. I am bruised and scratched a little, perhaps; but that is of no consequence."

The position of Colonel Wilder was a little embarrassing. This girl, whom he had treated so lightly and contemptuously, had saved his life, and he, man of the world as he was, did not know what to say to her. Fortunately his son rode up at that moment, and, in response to his inquiries, the colonel related the adventure.

"Yes, it was very well done," he said, as he noticed the admiring and affectionate glance that Fred bent upon Dove-eye. "She is accustomed to that sort of thing, no doubt; but that does not lessen my obligation. I have some presents that I brought for the Arapahoes, and I will give her something."

Fred blazed up, and would probably have made a sharp reply, if he had not been interrupted by the Crow chief, who came with the information that there were some strange Indians within sight of the camp.

A horse was procured for Colonel Wilder, and another for Dove-eye, and all set out toward the camp, except those of the Indians who were engaged in collecting the meat, and they soon followed.

"Father," said Fred, as they rode together, "you ought not to speak of offering presents to Kate Robinette. My wife, that is to be, does not care for beads and red cloth."

"Kate Robinette? Ah! I had forgotten that story. Do you really believe it? Well, it is no matter. She is a savage, and always will be."

"She is not a savage. If she were, I am sure that she will not always be."

CHAPTER XIV.
DIFFICULT NEGOTIATIONS.

The Indians who had been seen from the camp were Arapahoes, in pursuit of Dove-eye and the companions of her flight. Their chief was well enough acquainted with the reputation of both Old Blaze and Silverspur to know that they would not easily be caught, and he had determined to take enough men to follow them, if necessary, into the heart of the Crow nation. The pursuers, therefore, were a war-party, numbering nearly two hundred of the best braves of the Arapahoes, a truly formidable array to the Crows and their white friends, if their intentions should prove to be hostile.

Their inclinations were by no means peaceable. They halted on perceiving the Crows, and sent forward scouts to ascertain who and how many they were. When the scouts returned with the report that it was a band of Crows, accompanied by a small body of soldiers, they made preparations to attack, supposing that the Crows and their white allies were coming south to punish the Arapahoes for their last raid into the Crow country. They were a little fearful of coming into collision with Uncle Sam; but there was such a fine opportunity for obtaining scalps and plunder, that almost any excuse would serve them.

They were anticipated, however, by Colonel Wilder, who sent forward Lieutenant Rawlings and one of his men, with a flag of truce, to explain the objects of the expedition.

The messengers halted within a short distance of the Arapahoes, and made signs of amity, which were responded to by Black Horse, who rode out to meet them, accompanied by several warriors. The lieutenant informed them, in the bombastic style supposed to be necessary in dealing with Indians, that their great father in Washington had sent one of his war-chiefs for the purpose of persuading them to make peace with the Crows. The Crows, he said, were anxious for peace, and their head chief had come, accompanied by a number of his wisest warriors, to make peace with the Arapahoes. He concluded by inviting Black Horse to visit the camp of the white chief, who had brought a great many presents for his people.

The Arapaho chief replied evasively. He feared that there was some hidden motive under this invitation, and he wished to find out what it was before giving a positive answer. Besides, he was in pursuit of some fugitives, whom he was very anxious to overtake, and he did not wish to be delayed unless he was sure of gaining. He was anxious to make peace with the Crows, he said; but he was then traveling with a particular object, which he ought to accomplish before attending to any other business. He would like to know whether the lieutenant had seen two white men riding toward the Crow country, accompanied by an Indian girl and a negro.

Lieutenant Rawlings replied that he had seen them, and that they were even then in the camp of the white men and the Crows.

Black Horse was rejoiced at receiving this intelligence, though he maintained that stolid gravity of demeanor which permitted no trace of emotion to be seen. He thought that he perceived an opportunity to capture the fugitives, as well as to destroy the party of Crows and white men, and reap a rich harvest of scalps and plunder. He had warriors enough to defeat them; but he was not willing to risk their lives in a fair fight, as long as there was a chance to accomplish his object by stratagem. He commenced to negotiate, therefore, with a view to future treachery.

He was afraid, he said, both of the white men and the Crows. The white men had fought with the Crows against the Arapahoes, and he had reason to believe that they were his enemies. For himself, he was a simple and straightforward man, who was incapable of any treachery; but the Crows were known to be tricky, and he feared that the white men were not any more honest than they ought to be. His duty to his people compelled him to be on his guard against treachery, and it would be nothing more than fair, he thought, that he should be accompanied, on his visit to the white chiefs camp, by as many warriors as he would find there.

Lieutenant Rawlings contended against this proposition to the best of his ability, and protested the sincerity and peaceable intentions of the white men and the Crows; but Black Horse argued the point so mildly, rationally and plausibly, that the lieutenant was finally obliged to agree to his conditions. Having learned from him the numbers of the Crow warriors and white soldiers, Black Horse dismissed him, promising to visit the camp within an hour.

When the lieutenant returned and reported the result of his mission, he was blamed by his commander for the concessions that he had made. There was, also, a general feeling of distrust and uneasiness in the camp concerning the expected visit. Old Blaze did not hesitate to declare that treachery was intended by the Arapahoes, and that they ought not to be allowed to enter the camp. The Crow chief shook his head solemnly, and directed his warriors to put their weapons in good order. Silverspur was also gloomy, and made such preparations as he could, to meet the worst that might happen. Colonel Wilder declared that, as the Arapahoes had been invited to come in equal numbers, they must be allowed to do so. He was there for the purpose of making peace, and must not be frightened from his object by suspicion or possible danger. At the same time, he would be on his guard, and would employ all the means in his power to avert a collision and prevent treachery.

Within the hour the Arapahoes came in sight, approaching the camp. Their numbers and appearance, when they were near enough to be carefully observed, were not calculated to disarm suspicion. The Crows and whites did not number more than seventy-five fighting men; while the Black Horse had brought with him at least a hundred of his best warriors, all completely armed and in fighting trim. They were allowed to enter the camp without question, as preparations had been made to give them a warm reception in case of treachery.

"My red brother has brought a great many of his young men," suggested Colonel Wilder, when the chiefs had seated themselves on the ground. "The Crows and their white brothers have not so many warriors."

"The young white chief said that there were so many here;" but Lieutenant Rawlings protested that he had made no such statement.

"Black Horse does not pretend to be good at counting," superciliously replied the Arapaho. "A few warriors more or less are of no consequence. Why should the white chief care? If he does not wish to harm the Arapahoes, he need not ask to have as many warriors as they have, and he knows that they have no wish to harm his people."

Colonel Wilder let the subject drop, not deeming it of sufficient importance to allow it to disturb the "talk," and negotiations for peace were opened. But there was a difficulty at the outset.

In the group of Crows and white men were Old Blaze and Silverspur, and among the Arapahoes was the trader, Silas Wormley. Old Blaze was recognized by Black Horse, who had seen him when a prisoner in the Arapaho village, as well as on previous occasions. He had no doubt that the companion of the hunter was Silverspur, whom he knew by reputation. Silas Wormley, since his arrival, had been sharp-sighted enough to catch a glimpse of Dove-eye and Jose, whose presence he had duly reported to the chief. Assured that the fugitives were within his reach, Black Horse devoted his first efforts to gaining possession of them. Without going into particulars, he stated that they had stolen into the Arapaho country, where they had done a great deal of damage, and that he was in pursuit of them. He proposed, before proceeding to talk of peace, that these offenders should be delivered up to the Arapahoes, to be dealt with as they should see fit.

"Is this one of the men?" asked Colonel Wilder, pointing to Silverspur.

The chief nodded assent.

"He is my son."

"Are not all the white people children of the white chief?" sarcastically inquired Black Horse.

"His mother was my wife. You can not expect me to give up my son to be killed, when he has committed no crime deserving of death."

"Give us the other man, then—give us the Burnt Face," said Black Horse, who was willing to temporize, in order to gain time to carry out a little stratagem that he had planned.

"What has he done?"

The chief could allege nothing against Old Blaze, except that he aided Silverspur in carrying off an Arapaho girl.

"I will tell you what he has done," replied the colonel. "You captured him when he was hunting near your village, doing you no harm, and you released him of your own accord. You had no right to capture him, and you have no right now to reclaim him."

"At least we can claim the girl," said the chief, after casting an anxious glance at the plain behind him. "Will you give her to us?"

"What claim have you upon her? She is not an Arapaho."

"Not an Arapaho!" The chief started, astonished at this unexpected rebuff. "Does the white chief know what he is saying? Why does he say that she is not an Arapaho?"

"She is a Crow. She was stolen from the Crows many years ago. She is the adopted child of this chief"—pointing to Bad Eye. "She was his brother's daughter."

The countenance of Black Horse fell. He knew that it would be useless to deny this fact.

"I begin to be afraid," he said, "that you will not give us the horses that were stolen from us by these people."

"You shall have your horses, though I do not believe that they were stolen. Now let us talk of other matters. I have come to try to make peace between the Arapahoes and the Crows, and have brought presents for you."

Suspicious circumstances were transpiring in the mean time, indicating the nature of the little stratagem that had been planned by the Arapaho chief, and explaining the reason for his backward glances across the plain.

The Arapaho warriors, instead of scattering about the camp, to gratify their curiosity, and to pick up such loose available articles as they could lay their hands on, as was the custom of Indians on the plains at friendly talks, had kept in a body, had maintained a stolid gravity of demeanor, and had watched every movement of their chief and of all about the camp.

It soon became evident, also, that their numbers were increasing. On a neighboring elevation, and in the timber that bordered the creek adjoining the camp, were bodies of Arapahoes, from which small squads detached themselves now and then, and sauntered leisurely toward the camp, where they mingled with those who were already there.

These circumstances did not escape the keen eyes of the Arapaho chief, who became bolder and more impudent as he noticed the arrival of his reinforcements and the near approach of the rest of his band.

"The Arapahoes are not fools," he said, in reply to Colonel Wilder. "They make war or peace when they please, without asking the advice or assistance of the white men."

Colonel Wilder colored with indignation. He began to perceive that this Indian meant treachery and mischief, and he was not a man who could brook an insult from a savage.

"If my red brother does not wish to make peace," he said, "he can go as he came. The Arapaho has not done as he promised to do. He said that he would bring no more warriors than were here; but he has brought many more, and his young men are even now coming into the camp. I can not allow this."

"The white men tell us that we have a great deal of curiosity," replied Black Horse. "I suppose they speak the truth. My young men always wish to see and hear every thing."

"They must be sent back. As many warriors as we have may remain; but the rest of the band must remove a mile from our camp."

Black Horse was silent.

"Let the Arapaho answer. Is he willing to make peace, or does he still wish for war?"

"Is the white chief a coward?" contemptuously replied Black Horse. "Is he afraid of two or three poor Indians? Let him give us our presents, and then we will talk about peace."

Colonel Wilder made no response to this audacious demand.

"He must give us our presents," continued Black Horse, "and he must give up our prisoners, who have taken refuge in his camp."

"When peace is made, the presents will be distributed, and not before. There are no prisoners here who belong to the Arapahoes. If the chief does not wish to make peace, the way is open, and he can go as he came."

"We must have our presents and our prisoners."

A child could have seen that a collision was inevitable. Black Horse, with his tomahawk resting on his knee, and his rifle at his side, was haughty and overbearing, and glanced around at his warriors, as if conscious of his superior strength. The warriors, for their part, were collected in a firm phalanx. Their outward demeanor was calm and apparently indifferent, but their eyes, burning with revenge and thirst for blood and spoil, were fastened on their chief, as if waiting for the signal to commence the slaughter. Their teeth were clinched tightly, their muscles were strained as if for a spring, and their left hand held their rifles, while the right grasped the tomahawk or the battle-ax.

On the other side was the same calmness of demeanor, which gave little token of the excitement that was boiling within. The Crow warriors were ready and anxious to be let loose at their antagonists, notwithstanding the disparity in numbers, and behind their commander were drawn up the twenty dragoons, standing at a rest, with their carbines ready for instant action. Bad Eye, whose glance took in every thing that passed, had his weapons within reach, and Colonel Wilder kept his hand within his bosom, where it played nervously with the butt of a pistol.

Silverspur, who smelt blood in the air, had formed a plan of his own, which he meant to carry into effect upon the first outbreak of treachery. He had gradually and almost imperceptibly edged his way toward the Arapaho chief, until he was almost near enough to touch him. As he watched him closely, he perceived that there was a whistle in the end of the handle of his tomahawk, and he had no doubt that that whistle would give the signal for the onset, if any should be given. While appearing to have all his attention concentrated upon the speakers, he carefully kept one eye upon Black Horse and his tomahawk.

"What you ask is entirely out of the question," said Colonel Wilder, in reply to the last demand of the Arapaho chief. "If you have no better terms to offer, you may go, and take your warriors with you."

"The Arapahoes come as they please, and go as they please. They have not learned to obey the commands of the white men."

"If you will not have peace, you shall have war to your heart's content."

"Then let it be war!" exclaimed the chief, as he quickly raised his whistle to his lips.

But it did not sound. Before it reached his lips, Silverspur seized him, and, exerting all his strength, jerked him from among his warriors, into the ranks of the opposite side. Old Blaze, who had divined the intentions of his friend, caught the chief by the arms, and held him tightly; while Silverspur, grasping him by the scalp-lock, flashed his keen hunting-knife before his throat.

"Hold!" exclaimed the young man, as the Arapahoes were handling their weapons, uncertain whether to commence the attack. "If a shot is fired, or if a man moves from his place, your chief dies that instant!"

The position of the Arapahoes was by no means such as Black Horse had expected it to be. Their chief was in the power of their adversaries, liable to be killed at the first hostile movement they should make, and he had been seized before he was able to give them the signal for the onset. Before them was the line of dragoons, with carbines leveled and cocked, and all around them were clustered the Crow warriors, with rifles to the shoulder and arrows on the string. The Arapahoes saw that they had lost the advantage of surprise and the first attack, and were willing to make terms.

Colonel Wilder took the word where his son had left off.

"Leave the camp!" he said. "Draw off, every man of you, a mile from the camp, and take with you the warriors on the hill and in the timber yonder, and your chief will be safe. If you go peaceably, and do as I tell you, the chief will be released as soon as you reach your own camp. If you do not"—pointing at the leveled guns behind him—"you see that we have the advantage of you."

The Arapahoes hesitated a few moments, consulted a little with each other, and then sullenly returned in a body to their own camp.

Colonel Wilder read Black Horse a severe lecture upon his treacherous conduct, to which the Arapaho listened in silence, and released him when a scout reported that his warriors had all reached their former location.

CHAPTER XV.
KNIFE TO KNIFE.

Although the whites and the Crows had been saved from imminent peril, and probably from destruction, by Silverspur's prompt and decisive action, they were by no means safe from their enraged adversaries. It was to be supposed that Black Horse, indignant at the discovery and defeat of his treacherous scheme, would not be willing to abandon his enterprise without an effort. As the Arapahoes largely outnumbered their opponents, and were stimulated by the desire for plunder as well as revenge, it was reasonable to expect an attack upon them.

Colonel Wilder and Bad Eye, therefore, hastened to make preparations to repel their assailants. The wagons were so placed as to form a corral within which the horses were secured, and around this all were set at work to dig and throw up a breastwork. As the attack might be expected at any moment, they worked with a will, and the camp was soon placed in a fair condition for defense.

It was useless to think of retreating, as they were encumbered with wagons. The Arapahoes could easily overtake them, and might destroy them on the march.

Although the afternoon wore away without an attack, scouts reported that the Arapahoes were still in sight, and Colonel Wilder ordered the work of fortification to continue, until he believed the camp to be strong enough to resist an assault.

"The governor has rushed us pretty hard," said Silverspur, when the work was pronounced finished, and he threw himself on the ground to rest. "That is always the way with these military men. They want to build a fort at every step they take."

"He's right about it this time, sartin," replied Old Blaze. "The 'Rapahoes are more'n two to our one, and I don't know any red-skins that I hadn't ruther fight. Did ye notice those warriors that came with Black Horse?"

"Yes. They were a fine-looking set of men."

"No finer anywhere. Every man of 'em nigh onto six feet high, straight as a pine, soople as a painter, and jest built up a-purpose fur fightin'."

"They are, certainly, the best-formed and the most athletic Indians I have seen on the plains."

"Kerlectic! I don't adzackly swaller that word; but, if thar's any kerlectic red-skins livin', it's them. Why, boy, the Crows are puny alongside of them, and the crook-legged Comanches ain't worth shucks off thar hosses. How clean they all war! and how keerfully they war painted and 'iled!"

"They would be dangerous fellows in a close fight. I should dislike to meet one of them in a hand-to-hand tussle."

"They're powerful tough customers in a skrimmage, sartin. We would all have been chawed up afore this, ef thar game hadn't been bust into jest as it was. Thar'll be a right sharp tussle, I've a notion, afore we've done with 'em."

"I don't suppose that they mean to give up what they came for."

"Not a bit of it. They came arter Dove-eye, and they came arter you and me. They hev got a notion of the colonel's plunder, too, and Crow skelps and white skelps are what they're allers wantin'. They mean to hev some of those things, boy, or bust thar gizzards a-tryin'! Hullo! What's the matter now? Are the cusses comin' at us?"

There had been one lack in the camp. There was enough meat and enough ammunition; but Colonel Wilder, with the forethought of a soldier, saw that it might be necessary to stand a siege, in which event a scarcity of water would be a serious inconvenience. The creek was near at hand; but they would be cut off from it in case of attack, and a supply must be secured before the appearance of the enemy.

He sent a squad of dragoons to the creek, with a guard of Crow Indians, to get water to fill all the vessels that were available for that purpose. Twice they went and returned in safety; but, the third time, while they were filling their buckets, a party of Arapahoes, who had been lurking in the timber, rose from their ambush, and poured into them a deadly fire. Three of the soldiers were killed outright, and one was severely wounded. The Crows, after an ineffectual attempt to make a stand, were driven back, with their white companions, toward the camp. The Arapahoes pursued them at once, and, as they were incumbered with their wounded comrade, their progress was slow and difficult.

This was the disturbance that had attracted the attention of Old Blaze. There was a call for volunteers, to go out and bring in the party, and there was no lack of men for the service. Silverspur and Old Blaze headed a number of Crows and white men, who leaped over the breastwork, and hastened to the rescue of their friends. They soon drove back the pursuing party, but found that their work was not half done. The Arapahoes came pouring out of the timber, and in a few minutes the whole plain was swarming with them, closing in upon the little band, and blocking up the path to the fort.

There was nothing for Silverspur and his party to do, but cut their way through their enemies, and they set at work to do so, with the courage of desperation. Facing to front and rear, with the wounded in the center, they fought each way, gradually nearing the fort. But the number of their enemies increased, and the Arapahoes, attacking violently with guns, arrows, lances and war-clubs, gave them no rest, and threatened to exterminate them.

They would be overwhelmed, unless they should receive succor from the camp, and against this the wily chief of the Arapahoes had provided, or thought he had provided, by sending a strong force to attack the camp on the other side. But Colonel Wilder, relying on his intrenchments to repel this assault, detached a party to sally out on the side next the creek, to the assistance of his son. They attacked so vigorously, that the Arapahoes were surprised and scattered, and Silverspur took advantage of the few moments of breathing time that were thus given him, to get his men within the breastwork.

Even then he accomplished his task with difficulty. The Arapahoes quickly rallied, and turned upon their foes with renewed fury; striving to enter the camp with them. In this they were nearly successful, and the assault upon the other side of the camp received at the same time a fresh impetus.

If the attack had hitherto been desperate, it was now the extreme of desperation. Half the dragoons were killed or wounded, together with a number of the Crows, and the Arapahoes fought with such bravery and fury, that their antagonists, although aided by the breastwork, found it nearly impossible to keep them out of the camp. The contest quickly became one of hand to hand and foot to foot, and Old Blaze's estimate of the strength and agility of the Arapahoes was fully confirmed. Guns and bows were soon thrown away, and even lances were discarded. The struggle was continued with war-clubs, tomahawks and knives, and even with teeth and nails, while the ground within and without the breastwork became slippery with blood.

Silverspur, by the most arduous exertions, kept his assailants out of the camp; but Colonel Wilder was less successful on his side, his men being gradually beaten back, until the Arapahoes came pouring in over the breastwork. The gallant old officer rallied them for a resolute charge, and dashed into the midst of the enemy, firing his pistols right and left, and opposing his sword to their battle-axes and tomahawks.

The blade of his sword was soon broken against the tough handle of a club, and, while he was thus disarmed, an athletic warrior, no less a personage than Black Horse himself, rushed upon him, seized him by the throat and bore him to the ground.

With tomahawk upraised, the chief was about to dash out the brains of his foe, and the next moment would have been the last of Colonel Wilder, had it not been for the prompt interposition of Dove-eye, who, having picked up a battle-ax, rushed in, and served the chief as he had expected to serve the officer. With the assistance of one of the Crows, she dragged the Colonel out of the *mêlée*, while the Arapahoes made a rush for the body of their chief, picked it up, and carried it over the breastwork. At the same time the Crows and white men charged so vigorously, that the camp was soon cleared of enemies.

The yells and wailing cries that followed told the Arapahoes that their chief had fallen, and they soon drew off, to the great relief of the defenders of the camp. As they went, they carried with them their dead and wounded, a proceeding which their foes were unable to prevent, although some of them would have been willing to prevent it.

The Crows and the few remaining white men were so exhausted by the deadly and protracted struggle that they were glad to throw themselves on the ground and rest, even before they could attend to their wounded and count up their losses. When these came to be considered, all was sadness and gloom in the camp; for many had fallen, and scarcely any had escaped wounds or scratches. No one believed that it would be possible to withstand another assault; but it was hoped that the death of Black Horse would prevent their enemies from attempting another.

This hope proved to be well founded; but the Arapahoes were not willing to abandon the scalps and the plunder for which they had fought so desperately, and which they yet hoped to gain. Relying on their superior numbers, they surrounded the camp, guarding all the approaches, and keeping up such a fire that the defenders could not show their heads above the breastwork. The latter, as long as they were not called upon to resist another assault, were contented to keep quiet, to bind up their wounds, and to prepare some food to strengthen their bodies.

Fred Wilder said nothing concerning Dove-eye's achievement to his father; but it was not long before the latter brought up the subject.

"I had never believed," said the old officer, "that I would be compelled to praise a woman for the possession of a quality which is supposed to belong specially to men; but it is certain that this—a—young woman has shown remarkable courage and presence of mind. She has saved my life twice this day, and I believe that she saved the lives of all of us who are still living. Those bloodthirsty Arapahoes were pressing us very hard, and I fear that they would have captured the camp, if it had not been for the death of their chief."

"I hope," replied Fred, "that she will not again be called upon to use those qualities during this campaign, as it is too dangerous employment for my intended wife. But there are two other qualities which I am afraid she will be obliged to display, together with the rest of us—patience and endurance."

Those qualities were, indeed, greatly needed in the camp; for the night wore away, and the next day and the next night, without any relaxation on the part of the Arapahoes of their strict watch and ward about the beleaguered garrison, who were obliged to keep cautiously on the alert. It was evidently their design to accomplish by siege and starvation the object which they had not effected by open assault. To add to the troubles of the besieged, their supply of water began to give out, although it was used as sparingly as possible.

On the morning of the third day it was entirely exhausted, and the pains of thirst began to be seriously felt in the little band. They were thinking of attempting at all hazards, to cut their way through their foes, when the keen eyes of Old Blaze caught sight of some objects at a distance, moving over the plain. Colonel Wilder examined them with his telescope, and pronounced them to be a body of white men. The American flag was hoisted, with the union down, as a signal of distress, and the moving objects soon began to verge toward the camp. The Arapahoes saw them coming, and, after sending scouts to ascertain who they were, speedily and prudently decamped.

The arrivals proved to be a large force of trappers, led by Captain Benning, who rode up to the camp in great glee, joyfully welcomed by the rescued band.

CHAPTER XVI.
CONCLUSION.

Benning offered to pursue the retreating Arapahoes; but Colonel Wilder, who had tried their mettle, thought it would be the better course to leave them alone for the present and his opinion prevailed.

As the trappers were on their way to Benning's rendezvous in Green river valley, Colonel Wilder and the Crows determined to accompany them. Those of the wounded who were unable to walk were placed in the wagons, and the entire cavalcade took up the line of march toward the north.

Captain Benning was overjoyed at meeting Silverspur, who had aided him in rescuing his wife, then Flora Robinette, from the Blackfeet and the Arapahoes, and he was greatly pleased at discovering her sister Kate, who had been so long lost that her existence was nearly forgotten. The two friends beguiled the way by relating their adventures, none of which were more strange and exciting than Silverspur's pursuit of Dove-eye.

Colonel Wilder rode and conversed with Dove-eye during part of the journey, and Fred, when he saw him thus engaged, considerately kept away from him, believing, as was consistent with his own experience, that the girl of his choice needed only to be known to be appreciated.

The old gentleman could not help being respectful and friendly to her who had twice saved his life, and it was evident to Fred that he watched her with a growing interest. The more he saw her and talked with her, the more apparent became her good qualities. In fact, he was rapidly becoming convinced that she was not entirely savage, and that it would be possible to reclaim and civilize her. Before the journey was ended he came to the conclusion that it would not be at all difficult to reclaim and civilize her.

Fred only once rallied him upon his attentions to Dove-eye, merely for the purpose of getting an inkling of his real feelings with regard to her.

"She saved my life," replied the colonel. "She saved it twice, and I have no doubt that she saved the lives of us all. It is only just that I should be kind to her. Between you and me, she would be the right kind of a wife for a man who expected to live in the wilderness. She could take care of herself, and of her husband too, if necessary."

The young gentleman made no reply to this speech; but his thought was, "the governor is coming around."

Old Blaze was restrained by no motives of delicacy from expressing his opinion.

"Tell ye what, colonel," he said; "that gal is the right grit. She totes a true heart and a stout one. She was born to be a queen—that's whar it is."

The journey was accomplished safely and pleasantly, the party being too large to fear interruption by the Indians. When they reached the rendezvous, Kate Robinette was made known to her sister Flora, who had previously, during her captivity among the Arapahoes, considered and treated her as a sister. When she learned that her Indian sister was really her own elder sister, her joy was unbounded, and her affection displaced itself in all manner of extravagant demonstrations.

When Colonel Wilder saw Kate Robinette laughed over and cried over by her sister, who was undoubtedly white, and who called Bad Eye "uncle" as naturally as if he had not been a Crow chief, he began to doubt whether Dove-eye did not have white blood in her veins, and soon came to the conclusion that she was all white. Thereafter he addressed her as "Kate" and "Miss Robinette," and was as courteous to her as if she had been a fashionable damsel fresh from the "settlements."

"Now that sister Kate is found," said Flora, when everybody had got over the novelty of the discovery, "it is time that we should devise a plan by which I can divide father's property with her. I have no doubt that he would have divided it, if he had known that she was alive, and I am sure that there is enough for both of us. Besides, she is the eldest child, and has the best right to it."

"There is no necessity for any division," remarked Bad Eye. "You need not suppose that I, a white man, and a trader by education, have lived so many years among the Crows without making some use of the advantages of my position. On the contrary, I have had a splendid opportunity to amass a fortune, and have not entirely neglected it. I have trapped and traded until I have laid by a considerable sum, part of which is in the hands of Captain Benning, and the rest is mostly in St Louis. I intend that Kate shall have it all, and she will find, when it is gathered together, that she is not much behind her sister."

It could not be that Colonel Wilder was influenced by the discovery that Kate Robinette was an heiress. He had a great respect for wealth and position, but was no worshiper of property. It is certain, however, not only that his demeanor toward her entirely changed, but that he really gave his consent to her marriage with Fred.

"That is, my son," he proceeded to qualify, "after you have taken her to the East and kept her at school a few years. Education will soon polish her."

"Do you think I could allow the ducks and turkeys of the settlements to laugh at my wild bird?" asked Silverspur. "Do you think I could be separated from her a few years, or a few months? She is sufficiently polished, and no one can educate her better than her husband."

Fred had his way, and was married to Kate Robinette, without objection by any person. He entered into a partnership with Captain Benning as a fur trader, in which business both were remarkably successful. Kate's brains and will soon made amends for the deficiencies of her education, and, when she accompanied her husband to St. Louis, no one who was not acquainted with her story would have supposed that the greater part of her life had been spent among savages.

Bad Eye returned to his tribe, being resolved, as he had often declared, to live and die a Crow.

A short time after the foregoing events, Colonel Wilder led a detachment of troops and a band of Crow warriors against the Arapahoes, who were badly defeated and compelled to sue for peace.

Old Blaze continued in the employ of his friend Silverspur, when his vagrant propensities did not compel him to seek other occupation, and never ceased to regret that he had not shot "that tradin' chap."

THE END.